SAND, SALT, BLOOD

Edited by Elle Turpitt

All rights reserved. No part of this publication may be reproduced, stored in or introduced into a retrieval system, or transmitted in any form, or by any means (electronic, mechanical, photocopying, recording or otherwise) without the prior permission of the publisher. Any person who does any unauthorised act in relation to this publication may be liable to criminal prosecution and civil claims for damages.

The following is a work of fiction; names, characters, businesses, places, events and incidents are fictitious. Any similarities to actual persons living or dead, events, places and locations is purely coincidental.

This edition first published 2023 – also available as an ebook

Paperback ISBN: 9798391793540

© 2023 Sliced Up Press.

Web: sliceduppress.com / Tumblr: tumblr.com/sliceduppress

Cover art courtesy of Ellen Avigliano at imaginariumarts.com

Introduction © Elle Turpitt, *Adrift (Upon a Sea of Apathy)* © Christopher Sartin, *Nothing That Doth Fade* © Ariel Dodson, *Holden Ledge* © Miranda Johansson, *Undone* © Max Turner, *Swallow the Ocean* © Daphne Fama, *osedax* © Marisca Pichette, *The Odd-yssey* © Davis Walden, *No Ghosts Here* © A.J. Van Belle, *And In Her Eyes, The End* © Melissa Pleckham, *The Aequor* © H.M. Lightcap, *The Truth is As Intimate As The Teeth That Bit Off Your Legs First* © Elizabeth R. McClellan, *Fishing License* © Grace Daly, *Living Death Beneath The Waves* © H.V. Patterson, *Uncharted* © JP Relph, *Aqua Warrior Witches Save Our Water!* © Alicia Hilton, *Save for Joy* © Noah Lloyd, *A Void, Suspended With That Which Cannot Be Stars* © Taliesin Neith, *Wake* © Lucas Olson, *The Tide Will Bring Thee Home* © Dai Baddley, *I Float* © Gerri Leen

CONTENTS

Introduction
by Elle Turpitt p8

Adrift (Upon a Sea of Apathy)
by Christopher Sartin p13

Nothing That Doth Fade
by Ariel Dodson p14

Holden Ledge
by Miranda Johansson p28

Undone
by Max Turner p43

Swallow the Ocean
by Daphne Fama p56

osedax
by Marisca Pichette p65

The Odd-yssey
by Davis Walden p68

No Ghosts Here
by A.J. Van Belle p84

And In Her Eyes, The End
by Melissa Pleckham p98

The Aequor
by H.M. Lightcap p106

The Truth Is As Intimate As The Teeth That Bit Off Your Legs First
by Elizabeth R. McClellan p118

Fishing License
by Grace Daly p121

Living Death Beneath The Waves
by H.V. Patterson p133

Uncharted
by JP Relph p147

Aqua Warrior Witches Save Our Water!
by Alicia Hilton p156

Save For Joy
by Noah Lloyd p157

A Void, Suspended With That Which Cannot Be Stars
by Taliesin Neith p167

Wake
by Lucas Olson p183

The Tide Will Bring Thee Home
by Dai Baddley p199

I Float
by Gerri Leen p213

Author Biographies p215

Editor Biography p222

Trigger Warnings p223

INTRODUCTION
Elle Turpitt

I love the sea.

It is terrifying. It is also beautiful.

I grew up in a coastal town, with a shingle (pebble) beach. We grew up on stories, reminded often of how easily the sea could turn. The stories were underscored by how often we heard the booms of the lifeboats launching.

There's an island not far from that beach, a tiny thing just a short walk from the mainland when the tide is low. But the tide comes in very, very quick, and people are often trapped there, relying on the RNLI to help them get back.

UK readers will be familiar with the RNLI, and if, like me, they grew up on the coast, they probably had the importance of their work drilled into them from a young age. For those unaware, the Royal National Lifeboat Institution are an incredibly vital part of keeping people safe year-round. They respond to distress calls and rescue people, of course, but they also help train people on water safety and there are a number of very useful resources on their website (rnli.org).

My grandfather was a ship chandler. He passed before I was born, but as his job often involved going out to sea with the ships, even after his death the RNLI was my grandmother's favourite charity. She valued the work they did. When she passed, I wanted to find some way to honour her, and a sea horror anthology benefiting the charity came to mind. I was thrilled when Ben at Sliced Up Press responded to my pitch. Sliced Up Press were the first publisher I thought of and the first I approached, and it was clear I – and the anthology – were in great hands.

There's something else the RNLI do that has become more crucial and vital over the last few years: they assist boats crossing the channels when they get into trouble. This has drawn the ire of certain parts of the UK population, but it's important to note the RNLI is there for anyone who finds themselves in trouble out at sea. They are an amazing charity, and the evidence is clear – in 2021, they saved 408 lives. In my own hometown, they saved 4 lives, launching the lifeboats 41 times to rescue 54 people in total. Volunteers provide a 24-hour search and rescue service. Reading this anthology is, in a roundabout way, supporting the charity – so, from the bottom of my heart, thank you so much for picking this up.

To those who helped make this happen: a big thank you to S.H. Cooper, one of my first editing clients, for her consistent encouragement and for bringing me onboard as a co-editor for *A Woman Built By Man*. Thanks also to Joanne Askew, my very first client, Ellen Avigliano, my DHR co-admin, and Regi Caldart, my Esbat podcast co-host – working with all four of them over the last few years has been an absolute delight, and time and again they've been there for me, supported me, and pushed me with new experiences and challenges.

Thank you to everyone at Divination Hollow Reviews, friends of DHR, and the many people I've met through the blogging and horror communities.

And of course, to my family – this would not be possible without the constant support from my dad and my brothers, Aunt Jan, Uncle Bri and all my cousins. Saying goodbye to Gran was incredibly hard, but we got through together. To Nan and Ban, for always encouraging the little stories I used to write on post-it notes. Dad, especially, who fostered in me a deep love and respect for the sea. It's no exaggeration to say without my family I wouldn't have started and continued to both write and edit.

I received over 300 submissions for this anthology, and was overwhelmed not just with the high number, but the large amount of high quality, excellent submissions. Narrowing it down was a very difficult task, but the book you're holding contains the best. These are the poems and stories that consistently stuck with me, that I found myself thinking about long after reading, and that I prayed, when I sent out the acceptances, were still available.

Editing an anthology is an amazing experience, and I felt flattered so many entrusted their submissions to me. In these pages you'll find shipwrecks, sharks and sirens, and more, stories dealing with familial relationships, poems about the environment, and horrors hidden in the depths. Each one of these did something different with the idea of sea horror, and it's been amazing to see this go from a spark of an idea to honour my grandmother into the themes these writers tackled.

My hope is that after reading this anthology,

you'll never look at the sea the same way again.

And just a couple of last thanks – my partner, my rock, my absolute biggest supporter in every project I tackle. Couldn't do any of this without Rich's encouragement.

To another of my supporters, often found sleeping on my lap or begging for food when I was reading submissions: our little 2pac. I was so looking forward to taking snaps of this book with her, but not long before I sat down to write this, we had to say our goodbyes. The bestest cat, missed every day.

I never knew my grandad, but between Gran and my dad I've heard plenty enough stories to feel like I did. So, most importantly, because without my grandparents this never would have come about.

Sand, Salt, Blood was started in Gran's memory, to benefit a charity she always supported, because of Grandad George's job. This anthology is for them.

And thank you, reader, for picking this up. Now, don't forget your scuba gear, don't leave anything behind, and hope nothing malfunctions for you when you're down in the depths. Never forget: respect the sea, because if you don't, who knows what's waiting for you beneath those waves.

ADRIFT (UPON A SEA OF APATHY)
Christopher Sartin

Pestilence and mutiny
Cast them adrift
Upon an apathetic sea.

Their ship, a distant pyre,
Aflame with the hopes
And dreams of a new world.

With neither land nor star in sight,
Shanties became their compass
Whilst tall tales became their anchor.

But songs only soothe for a time
And tales only serve as maps
On the journey to madness.

For when their raft finally made shore
Only one man remained afloat,
Bathed in the blood of his companions.

NOTHING THAT DOTH FADE
Ariel Dodson

She knew it'd happened even before the announcement; could feel it sinking with the heart she thought she no longer had.

Of course it would happen to her.

Her first real holiday, a luxury cruise she could never have dreamed she would have been able to afford – it seemed like destiny catching up with her, like something from a Greek myth; an alternative life she could have had, might have had, dangled tantalisingly before her starving lips, then snatched away, while somewhere above the gods laughed.

If it had been Althea, no doubt the gods would have smiled and sent her on her merry way. But then that was always Althea. Or, rather, had been.

It was hard to believe sometimes that she had gone. She had loomed in such a gargantuan manner over the thoughts and ambitions of her poorer, plainer cousin for so long, Audra wasn't sure if she could ever believe it. Yet believe it she must, for she had been there at the time, had seen her go, had felt the last desperate grasp on life strain through Althea's brittle, angry fingers as they had clutched Audra's wrist like one final plea and, lastly, watched her eyes widen and fade as the final death pang gripped her, hard and painful, and she was gone, gone to somewhere else, first again as usual, except that this time, Audra didn't mind.

It had been almost hard to let go of her though, and irritating too, for Audra knew that, had the roles been reversed, Althea wouldn't have spent longer than a moment thinking of her poor dead cousin, no longer than she ever had during her life. Not from any ill will, of course – oh no, Althea had been generous and loving to a fault, and Audra hadn't been surprised when the aunts insisted she take the cruise tickets, for that's what Althea would have suggested herself. And Audra couldn't deny that it burned her more than a little to know it was true.

It had been wonderful, though. Even though she had remained in her cabin for meals, had hurried past the deck games, and spent hours in the darkened, rocking arms of a corner cinema seat, too shy and uncultured to dare talking to anyone, it had been wonderful. She had bought a new set of clothes before the trip, especially for it, and even though there had been no one to see her, swirling girlishly in front of the cabin mirror, she still felt like Bette Davis in Now, Voyager, ready for something unexpected and new to come along and change her life.

Well, she had certainly been right about that. The waters had been choppy since the first afternoon, although oddly there had been no wind, and nothing particular to suggest the onset of a storm. And yet it swelled the further they journeyed out to sea, until the night, last night, when it crescendoed to the point she had flung herself on her bed with the covers over her ears, trying to ignore the screams from the other passengers as they hurtled themselves along the corridor outside her door. She heard china breaking from somewhere in the distance, and supposed it was coming from the dining room, in which she had never set foot. Ironic then, wasn't it, that it was a table from that very room which had saved her, floating upside down like something from Alice's adventures, and allowing her to heave herself on to it, dripping wet and freezing and watching in terror as the ridged nose of the vessel sank slowly beneath the now quiet waters, like some enormous, silent sea beast.

Everything was gone, everything and everyone, and she didn't understand why she alone had been saved, if saved was the right term for one lonely woman, dripping in finery that still felt borrowed and was forming a puddle in the shallow recess of her refuge.

It was the longest night she had ever known, even longer than the final night with Althea, and it seemed oddly fitting that the only counting game she could think of to keep her mind away from the awfulness of her situation was to recall the drops she had measured out to Althea on that last, long night – one, two, three – then four, then five, then six. Oh, she had known exactly what she was doing; had seen the will, poking around one day in Althea's bedroom drawers on one of the visits expected to a sick relative, and she suggested then to the aunts that she become Althea's full-time carer. She hadn't had anything else to do at the time – her boring administrative job paid out a reasonably good redundancy when her employer had gone bust a few years ago, her only compensation for the years of soulless data entry into seemingly endless spreadsheets – and it would do Althea good to know that there was someone nearby who cared, who wasn't being paid for her duty. Not yet, anyway.

Would she have recovered? It was possible of course, for the illness wasn't terminal, but Audra had convinced herself without much trouble that she had been doing her cousin a favour. The wife of one of her bosses had suffered from exactly the same ailment, and it dragged out until the poor woman was a shadow of her former self. Would blonde, bubbly Althea have wanted friends and family to see her that way, or would she have preferred they remember her as she was, young and lovely and in her prime? If it had been Audra, she told herself, it would definitely have been the latter, and so she had not held back when it came time for the evening's dose, on the day she decided. The doctor had been lazy – it had been a serious illness after all, and this was one expected outcome. Why bother with the paperwork to investigate further?

It had all seemed so easy, so meant to be, and yet now–

The touch was sudden, cold and clammy, sliding past her ankle familiarly and then again, as if to make sure she had felt it.

Audra suppressed a scream, and drew her foot firmly into the small cavity of wooden underbelly.

There it was again. The table rocked menacingly as the water rippled beside her, the moonlight shining on a white ropelike creature slithering beneath the surface of the waves, sinking slightly then surfacing again, bumping against her precarious haven as if demanding it share sanctuary.

17

What was it? It didn't seem to be moving, and yet a sudden jerk from something deeper below the water forced it through, clearly no sea creature now, but a hand and arm, cold and dead, and the white staring eyes of the bloated face that followed identified the thing as one of the passengers. Audra remembered seeing her – she was one of those you couldn't miss, blonde and vivacious, a bit like Althea in fact, and Audra had noted her, a little jealously it must be admitted, for that very reason. Audra also remembered the diamond necklace the woman had worn, the same one hanging around her neck now, and she braced herself as she reached forward and grasped it, hard and firm, so it came away in her hand. What use would it be to the fish, she told herself even as she shuddered at her own action, and surely there was a tiny chance that she might be rescued?

    She cast a quick look again at the corpse as she slipped the jewel into her pocket, irrationally desperate to try it on but keenly aware her frozen fingers wouldn't oblige. The thing was sinking now, the icy eyes seeming to stare straight at Audra as if accusing her, the stiff arm last to disappear below the water, like one final, terrible wave for help. There was a ring there too, diamond and emerald it looked, and Audra couldn't help herself. She leaned forward, even as she grimaced, her will somehow forcing her freezing fingers to act. She could feel the hard metal, although she wasn't sure how she could force it over the bloated skin with no implements handy.

    She braced herself, one hand gripped as tightly as the cold would allow around the furthest table leg, while she stretched herself to pull with the other.

It was like a kick. The table flung her as if something had pushed it from beneath, throwing her face first towards the corpse so she could smell the dead breath. She screamed, half sliding into the water, and the stiff, clammy hand seemed suddenly strong on her fingers as if trying to pull her down. She screamed again, sure that the thing had grinned at her for one malevolent second before pulling again, hard and malicious, towards the depths.

Audra didn't know how she had held on.

The black water was like ice, and for just a second her face smacked it, submerging her briefly before the table bounced upright, intact once more, her stiff, frozen hand almost soldered to the leg in its desperate grip.

It was a few minutes before she could fully grasp what had happened, but the cold must be turning her head, for she could not possibly have seen what she thought she had seen, there below the water, white and voluminous and threshing like eels. She was sick there and then, retching over the side, the glitter of the ring, somehow now in her hand, shining like a tiny star on the water.

It must have lulled her to sleep for a little while, that tiny floating star, despite the hunger and the fear and the wet, biting cold, for she jolted awake suddenly, stiff and aching and so disorientated she almost capsized herself.

She was still there. Still alone on the water, surrounded only by moonlight and darkness and the mocking laugh of the bobbing waves.

There was no sign of any debris from the ship. It was as if the waters had swallowed it and its cargo whole, all except for her, spat out it seemed, rejected even by the ever hungry sea. Her eyes were swollen with the wind and the salt spray, and she realised suddenly how thirsty she was, falling for the desperate measure of trying the salt water more than once then spitting it out, knowing full well it was undrinkable.

She wiped her mouth carefully, her hands so cold she had forgotten the stolen weight of the heavy ring on her finger, grazing herself slightly with the stone as it brushed against her chin. That was something at least, for all the good it did her, for she'd very likely never see land or another person ever again.

It was beautiful though, and she admired it with a strange, empty satisfaction, rippling her fingers in front of her face like a child playing a game, so the jewel sparkled in the moonlight. Funny, it didn't look so much like an emerald now, more like a huge diamond staring back at her in a frozen tear, and the setting was different, for she recognised it, a round glittering egg embedded in a nest of tiny pearls and fenced by a golden ripple like a miniature crown. She knew this ring, for she had lusted after it many times herself in the past, and had felt the same weak triumph when she had slipped it from Althea's finger on that last, long night before she was gone.

It couldn't be. It couldn't be that one, for she had left it at home deliberately, jointly worried it might be stolen on the journey or that one of the ever industrious aunts might have accidentally found it when helpfully checking her packing. It had been missed – it was a valuable piece and utterly unique, for Althea's wealthy grandfather had commissioned it especially for her grandmother when he had asked for her hand. It had been passed down to Althea, of course, for Audra did not share those grandparents, much to her dismay. And yet, it had come to her, after all. Or so she had thought. What was this then? Where had it come from, and how had that woman obtained a ring so similar it could have been the same?

It came to her suddenly, the memory of the engraving on the band, and she rubbed her fingers along it unwillingly, thankful at last for the cold she hoped would prevent any further discovery. But her icy fingertips still identified the marks like feet on a well-known trail, one after the other, signifying a private love message from a family history that was not her own, and she did not need to read them to know what they said.

She didn't know how it happened then, whether it was her own fear or a jolt suddenly beneath her, but something jerked the table, knocking her hand and causing the precious ring to fly into the water with a silent, dignified plop.

She didn't even need to think about it, barely bothering to secure herself as she dipped her numb hand into the black, laughing waters again and again, as if somehow luck would favour her the same way it had rescued her and return the ring. It had been all the same to Althea – she had owned dozens of expensive rings, and she hadn't even worn this one very much, laughing at times about its old-fashioned heaviness and style. Surely then it belonged with Audra, who loved it and who had paid so dearly to obtain it?

But it was no use, like looking for a needle in a haystack as the saying went, and she was about to give up, her arm so cold it felt it might drop off, when she felt the graze of metal against her skin and peered hopefully again into the water, wondering if she was going a little mad to think that the sea might bequeath her the gift.

The moon was behind a cloud now, and it was difficult to see what went on below, her stiff fingers twitching crablike in the lapping waves, the hard surface still tapping her skin as if taunting her. She positioned herself more firmly, digging her knees into the wet, shallow basin and edging closer to the water, her hair loose now, the strand ends floating on the black liquid like seaweed. She could have been a mermaid looking back at herself.

The hand seized hers before she was aware of it, before she could cry out, a deathsure grip, pulling and tugging her down and down until her face was below the surface and she saw the body again, the dead blonde woman, her swollen hand fleshy and raw and fastened like a predator over Audra's own. Her hair was floating too, floating upwards towards Audra like mist, until she found her eyes and her mouth full of it. She opened them then, still below water and choking now in the wet-salt gasps and lack of air, while the corpse slowly raised its head so that the blue puffy face was right before hers, the equally blue eyes open and leering, and she saw Althea's face before her suddenly, smiling then laughing, and it was all Audra could do to heave herself upwards, back towards the air and the night and her bobbing haven, back before the shark that had just taken her hand with it came back to do any more damage.

She could see herself heaving as she nursed her wrist, her shoulders rocking in time to her fierce, drawn-in breaths, her shadow on the moonlit waves dancing heavily in rhythm with her anguish, the laughing water mocking her salt-crusted eyes that were too frozen to cry. She seemed to be standing outside of herself then, as if the moment was too traumatic to handle and she had somehow ejected herself temporarily from her own body in a defence mechanism, and was looking at herself from above. Perhaps too, the crisis had driven her just a little mad, for her shadow seemed to be multiplying now, twinning itself once, twice, then again and again as the waters writhed suddenly with a large, dark mass, now one, now several, and the waves began to separate as though expertly sliced by a knife as one, then two, then a dozen fins, cruel and keen, surfaced, drawn no doubt by the blood she imagined she still saw in the inky water, blood of the torn waves, her blood, as if they had now become one.

The creatures drew together, sleek and silent, then apart as they began to circle, the waves grinning now in a crown of dark blades. It was not a prize she desired and she drew herself together tightly, praying the table would not capsize, praying she could stem the flow of blood weakening her with every throb. It was too cold to hurt, too cold for her to feel anything, and as she seemed to re-enter herself she could not help but remember Althea's icy stare as she had administered the dose that night; one, two, three – then four, then five, then six. The amount had stunned her, and Audra had been aware of it even if she hadn't admitted it to herself at the time. She remembered gazing down at her cousin, her smile gentle and kindly as all the while she spooned the mixture into the still, open mouth, spooned the death knell in, knowing that Althea was still alive and alert behind the slow freezing taking hold of her nerves as the liquid flowed, spooned again and again fully aware that Althea would die knowing exactly who had killed her and was unable to say a word.

The jolt came again then, sudden and angry, as if it had heard her thoughts, and she had to flail clumsily like a seal on land to avoid being thrown overboard.

What was it? She was aware of trying to turn her head but being unable to do so, she was so cold and stiff.

Was it the sharks? Were they trying to force her off? Were they that intelligent?

There was a thumping now, close and steady, and she could not be sure whether it was coming from underneath the table or from the frenzied pounds of her own heart. Come out, come out, wherever you are. It was a game she and Althea played as children, and she didn't know why she should think of it now, why it suddenly seemed so important.

The second jolt was even fiercer, and if her handbag, which she had had the odd presence of mind to bring with her as the alarm had been rung, had not been slung around one of the legs and her own good arm slung around the bag, she would have been gone.

As it was, her legs hit the water with a slap, and she was terrified for a moment that the sharks had taken those too, for although she had heard the noise of her body hitting the water, she could feel nothing. How could she do it? How could she pull herself up with one hand, and that hand not even free, tangled as it was in the strap of the bag? Her expensive new bag, that she had so feared might be stolen.

She could feel herself blubbering, although her frozen face remained in a masklike grimace. She must be kicking, she was willing herself to kick, and where were they? The fins, the teeth, the sharks?

When the touch finally came she would have screamed, but her voice would allow it no more than her lips, and she could do nothing but scrabble as much as her icy body would allow, scrabble and writhe like a child splashing in a play pool, except that this was not playing, and the hand that gripped her ankle with a fierce, determined tug was definitely no shark.

She could do nothing, her chin fighting desperately to keep above the salt water that found its way into her ears, her eyes, her nose, and her frozen, silent mouth, her arms flailing frantically above her head in a last desperate plea that someone, somewhere, might be able to help her. But there was only the sharp cry of a gull from somewhere above, a mewling pierce like that of a cat or a baby, that broke the silence and glided over the water in a sleek predatory shadow. When she sensed the tug on her bloody wrist – more a physical jerk than any pain, for she was beyond feeling now – she was not surprised, for the dawn was starting to push back the darkness and everything must eat. Even that which was below.

They were pulling her from both ends now, the birds above and the hands below, more of them now, as if a mob was lurking below the surface, and, as her arm slipped free of the bag and her frozen eyes dipped finally beneath the water she could see them, the great mass of writhing bodies, grey and pulpy, the staring eyes fixed amidst the floating cloud of jewellery and coins that had followed them to their deaths, for the sea is greedy and indiscriminate.

They were tangled together like one huge body of conjoined parts, heads, arms and legs waving from all ends like some enormous, obscene sea creature from legend. They were staring at her, greedy and furious, as the valuables circled her, more rings, necklaces and brooches than she could have ever imagined, mocking her and her mutation, mocking her and her dying, as she had mocked Althea.

Was this to be her hell then? She and the shadow of Althea, forever joined as they always had been? She remembered again the glassy stare as her cousin had faced her, her helpless mouth open and waiting in her catatonic face as Audra had spooned in her death again and again; one, two, three – then four, then five, then six.

She would remember it forever.

The nearest body to her jolted then, the head snapped to as though suddenly awoken, the eyes not glassy now but angry and vengeful.

It was the blonde woman, the one who had reminded her of Althea, then suddenly it was Althea, the face fresh and suddenly beautiful, the smile genuine as it widened, broader and broader, delighted to see her as Althea always had been, social butterfly that she was. Audra stared back helplessly as the beautiful face suddenly greyed and flattened, the eyes black and empty now like pools of death, the smile unforgiving as the teeth opened and snapped, and Audra felt her body alive and alert for the last time as the water spooned into her silent cry – one, two, three, then four, then five, then six – and the crown of fins closed around her in a wet, sharp nest of pearls.

HOLDEN LEDGE
Miranda Johansson

A year or so back, Robin's mom had renovated her kitchen. She'd had the gas range taken out and replaced with a state-of-the-art induction stove; she'd gotten rid of the midcentury behemoth of a fridge. And she'd had new counters put in. Black granite, polished to a mirror sheen.

It was the counters Robin kept thinking about, as he did his best not to look at the sea.

The night was snowless and perfectly still. The water lay smooth and black, stars embedded in its surface like glittering chips of mica. It was the slack of the tide, and farther out to sea the top of Holden Ledge rose above the water's surface. The Ledge's highest points were a couple of promontories, curling inward around a cleft in which the shipwrecked yacht sat lodged, like a cigarette pinched between a giant's fingers.

It had been three days since the wreck appeared, and still no one knew where it came from or who owned it.

Robin sat at the rowboat's stern, hands stuffed in his jacket pockets, trying to stop his teeth from chattering. He was wishing he'd brought along a thermos of something—or better yet, that Clayton had never decided to drag him along on this stupid scavenger hunt in the first place. He could've been in bed right now.

"Man, you fucking owe me for this," he muttered.

Clay, who was at the oars, grinned. "What's the matter?" he asked. "You getting scared?"

"No," Robin said, pugnaciously. "But it's fucking cold."

"Really? This is, like, T-shirt weather to me."

Robin rolled his eyes. Clay meant it literally: he'd taken his jacket off and stuffed it underneath the thwart, even though it was cold enough that his breath came out in plumes. Clay was a good guy, but he had an unfortunate need to prove how tough he was, whether it be by weathering the November cold or rowing out to the wreck that everyone and their mother was telling ghost stories about. He'd developed it at some point during puberty, and it had gotten old fast.

"There's not gonna be anything there," Robin said. "You know that, right? The coast guard already searched, like, the entire thing."

"There's gotta be something," Clay replied. "I just wanna check it out. Bring back a souvenir or whatever before they tow it away." He grinned again. "You sure you're not scared, bro?"

"I'm not—"

Without warning, Clayton threw his weight to the side. The boat lurched horribly, and Robin yanked his hands out of his pockets to steady himself. He sat stiff as a board, holding on to the gunwales, until the boat's crazy rocking had subsided. "Asshole!" he barked breathlessly.

Clayton's shoulders were shaking with laughter. "You are such a pussy, dude!"

Robin's supposed fear of water was a favourite topic of conversation for Clay, but it was just bullshit. So he didn't want to pitch overboard into the icy sea. That didn't make him a pussy. It just meant he had a working brain.

Clay himself was not afraid of anything, least of all water. His dad John, who came from a long line of lobster fishermen, was a windburnt, taciturn guy who spent more time at sea than he did on land, and Clay had been on boats and ships since before he could walk. The sea did not bother him. But, okay, maybe Robin, whose family went road tripping for vacations rather than sailing, sometimes shivered a little at the thought of it. The cold, the pressure. The traps full of lobsters, clambering blindly over each other down there in the dark.

The noise of the oars sucking at the water was loud in the stillness. Ripples from the rowboat's passage spread and died on the dark surface of the sea, blotting out the stars, fraying the pale track of the moon. The wreck was looming closer, a darker shape against the night sky. The low tide only barely grazed the bottom of its keel.

Three nights ago, there had been a hell of a storm—a real batten-down-the-hatches-ass winter storm, the kind where you don't go outside if you can help it, because it feels like the frozen rain will scour the skin from your face. The kind where banshee winds scream about the eaves of your house, and you make damn sure the flashlights all have working batteries. During the night, a thirty-foot beech, torn up at the roots, had fallen on Jake Pittman's family's house. There had been a little drive for donations to help cover the reparation costs; Robin's parents pitched in with fifty bucks.

The next morning, the entire town had been glazed over with a thin layer of ice. The weather was bright and clear, and so cold that every breath sang in your teeth. And the wreck was there, serene and inscrutable, perched atop Holden Ledge.

The wreck was a yacht, sixty feet long, with the graceful lines of a pleasure craft and a hull made not of fiberglass but out of wood. It must have been beautiful, once, but it had had a rough journey. Now it was a sorry thing, waterlogged and festooned all over with barnacles—not just below the waterline, but all over, that was the weird part. As best as anyone could figure, it must've sunk at some point in the past, and remained on the seafloor until somehow the currents dislodged it and the storm deposited it neatly on the reef.

The coast guard had searched it and found nothing. No passengers, no logbooks. Any identifying marks on the vessel's hull had long since worn off. The wreck was unidentifiable.

After that it had been off to the races. Reporters had come from as far away as Boston to stand on the pebble beach and talk to their cameras, their coiffed haircuts whipping in the wind, the mysterious shipwreck artfully visible over their shoulders.

The media frenzy lasted for all of two days

before the news cycle moved on to bigger and better things. Now the beach was as desolate as ever, and the wreck was stuck in legal limbo while the authorities worked out what to do with it. And, in the meantime, Robin and Clayton were going to sneak onto it, to look for 'souvenirs'.

The Ledge was now less than thirty yards away. The wreck reared up, its railing skeletal in the darkness. Clay raised the oars, and the boat glided the rest of the way in silence. Even the thump of its keel striking stone was soft, as if it did not want to disturb the hush that lay over the reef.

Clay stood, pulled his jacket out from beneath the thwart, and stepped onto land. He held the boat by the breasthook while Robin followed, far less surefooted. Holden Ledge was a ridge of bald rock, slick with spray and algae, and Robin had to step carefully to avoid slipping as he approached the wreck. Behind him, the keel of the boat scraped against stone as Clay pulled it aground, and he cringed at the sound, harsh and loud and somehow unnatural in the stillness.

Clay caught up with him and handed him one of the flashlights, then clicked the other one on and let its beam glide across the flank of the wreck. As they stood side by side staring up at the barnacled hull, for a moment Robin thought he could sense in Clay a little of what he himself felt: tension, reluctance.

"Brandon Stanick told me there was a yacht just like this that went missing ten years back," Clay said, in hushed tones. "Owned by this married couple. They went out sailing and didn't come back. Someone found the lady, like, two weeks later. Just drifting.

Still had her life jacket on."

"What, alive?" Robin asked.

"Yeah, alive."

"Bullshit."

"Swear to God," Clay said. "Brandon said so. He said there was something wrong with her. Like she'd seen something that had made her go fucking crazy."

Robin glanced at him. Sure enough, the son of a bitch was grinning. So much for tension and reluctance. "Okay, dude," he said. "Let me guess—she talked about seeing ghosts or mermaids or whatever the fuck. And she killed an orderly and disappeared from the mental hospital without a trace. Then you'll point behind me and scream in terror or whatever. Really funny, classic bit."

Clay snickered. "So, are we doing this or what?"

Well, if he wasn't going to back down, neither was Robin. "Yeah."

They had to circle around to get onto the wreck, clambering on their hands and feet up the taller of the two promontories, which overhung the deck. Neither of them spoke. The silence seemed somehow difficult to challenge.

Their flashlight beams fell upon once-smooth wooden boards, now warped and rotting. Robin had hoped against hope that there'd be something on the deck they could just grab and leave, a life preserver or something, but no such luck. The deck was bare but for the barnacles. He lingered near the bow while Clay picked his way aft. There was an uneasy feeling in his stomach, and he turned his flashlight away, because he didn't like the way it made Clay's shadow splay hugely against the pilothouse.

The windows of the pilothouse were surprisingly still intact, but so scratched and cloudy as to be almost opaque. Clay pressed his face as well as his flashlight against one, trying to peer inside. Robin tried not to picture a face appearing on the other side, separated from Clay's by mere millimeters of plexiglass, a face with the bulging eyes of a dead fish, a face with fishhooks for teeth.

Scoffing, Clay turned away and tried the door instead. It opened with a low groan, making the hair on Robin's arms stand on end. A miracle, really, that the hinges hadn't rusted completely shut. Clay swept his flashlight once across the helm, then again across the ceiling, then stepped inside.

"See anything?" Robin called in a low voice.

"Jack shit," Clayton informed him soberly. "There's nothing in here."

Robin plucked up the courage to follow him, treading carefully, testing the boards of the deck before he put his weight on them. He stood in the doorway, illuminating the scene with his flashlight. Clay was squatting, rummaging through the storage spaces of the helm.

"Come on," Clay muttered. "There's gotta be something cool around here somewhere."

"There's not. I told you. The coast guard's been here already. If there was anything, they probably took it. Like, as evidence."

"Evidence for what? They're not cops, dude." Clay sat back, sighing, his wrists heavy on his knees. "Man."

"Look, let's just leave," Robin said. "We—"

Something creaked near the bow.

Robin whirled around, his heart in his throat, gripping his flashlight like a weapon. A gnarled, skeletal silhouette, towering and clawed, was not caught in its beam like he'd expected. There was nothing there.

"Stop being such a pussy," Clay said, contemptuously. "It was just the ship. It's, like, settling."

"Settling?" Robin said, giving him a sharp look. "Like, it's moving? Dude, we should not be here."

"It's not moving. I told you to stop being a pussy." Clay brushed past him and stepped back out onto the deck. His breath puffed in the air. "Let's go below decks."

Robin's stomach dropped. "Dude—"

"I just wanna take a look around," Clay said. "It'll take, like, five minutes." He gave Robin a withering sideways look. "You can stay up here if you're scared."

Robin stared at him for a moment. Then he scoffed. "Yeah," he said, gratified to hear he sounded braver than he felt. "Great idea. And then you'll, like, fall on a harpoon or something, and you'll be screaming for help, and I won't hear 'cause I'll have AirPods in."

Clay laughed. "Man, I hope there's harpoons down there. That would be fucking sick."

They searched the deck until they found the way down: a narrow stair with slick wooden risers disappearing into perfect darkness. Clay went down first, surefooted as a mountain goat, without so much as steadying himself with his hands, like he traipsed down deathtrap stairs every day. Robin, watching him go, felt a queasy twist in his stomach. He was thinking of the lightless deeps, where the lobsters crawled over each other.

Once, he had told Clay that the whole lobster-fishing thing seemed kind of unfair. "Like, here are these lobsters, just minding their own business, just looking for food," he'd said. "And bam, they walk right into a trap set by an animal with a brain, like, a million times bigger than theirs. They probably still haven't figured out what's going on by the time they're getting boiled."

Now, staring down into the dark belly of the yacht, Robin wondered. Were the lobsters really that mindless? Or did they have moments like this, where they stopped and stared into the jaws of danger and weighed the fear in their little lobster hearts?

But he wasn't going to stay up here. For one thing, what if something did happen to Clay? And, more importantly, if he didn't go, he'd never hear the end of it. That was one thing the lobsters probably didn't need to worry about. Nobody was going to brand one of them a pussy for not going in the trap.

And anyway, Robin didn't want to be left behind in the cold hush, alone with the dark mirror of the sea.

He took the stairs one step at a time, his shoulders hunched and his hands close to his body. Even though he lacked Clayton's effortless balance, he'd really rather not touch the algae-slick walls. He didn't want to touch anything down here. He just wanted to be gone.

He was almost at the bottom of the stairs when his foot slipped. Without thinking, he threw out a hand and steadied himself against the wall.

An instant later, he jerked it away. "What the fuck!" he cried, stumbling down the last couple of steps to the base of the stairs, where he tripped over his feet and fell on his ass.

"What?" Clay demanded, shining his flashlight on him. "What?"

There was a note of fear in Clay's voice which he could not quite disguise, but Robin was too horrified himself to feel any satisfaction about that fact. His skin was crawling all over. "The—the wall," he managed, wiping his palm on his jeans. "There's something wrong with the wall."

"'Wrong'? What do you mean, 'wrong'?"

Robin pushed himself to his feet, staring wild-eyed at the spot he'd touched. "I put my hand on it," he said, and pointed. "Right there. It's…"

Clay stepped in front of him and pressed a hand to the same spot. After a moment, he shuddered, and almost pulled away. He felt it too, then. Good. Maybe now he'd understand that they needed to get out of here.

"Cool," Clay whispered.

"Cool?" Robin hissed. He could hear the fraying, hysterical edge in his voice. "Clay, we gotta leave! It's…"

Clayton turned to look at him. That earlier fright, that crack in his facade, was gone, spackled over with bravado. "It's just, like, water moving against the hull. Or something."

37

"There's no waves," Robin whispered. "There's no wind. Clay, let's go."

"No," Clay said, in a hard, stubborn voice. "I wanna look around."

He started down the corridor, his expression sullen, shining his flashlight into the open doors of empty cabins. Robin remained at the foot of the stairs, hesitating. He glanced at the spot he'd touched. The flesh of his palm was still crawling. He had touched the wall only for an instant, but in that instant, what he had felt had not felt like the wreck settling, or like the sea lapping against its hull.

He was alone. Clay had disappeared from sight. Robin made a sound, a shamefully girlish whimper, and hurried after him.

He caught up with him near the stern, in a cramped galley full of empty yawning cupboards. Clayton stood next to a metal hatch set into the floor. By the glow of Clay's flashlight, Robin could see a short ladder leading down, and beyond it the inner curve of the hull. It was a hold or something, a space barely large enough to stand upright in, empty but for a foot or so of black water. Clay had a look on his face like he was seriously considering it.

"No," Robin heard himself saying. "Clay, please. You're not going down there."

Clay looked at him. His face, out of the beam of either of their flashlights, was shadowed; his eyes were like pools of dark water. "There might be something down there."

"There's nothing down there, moron! You can see that from here!"

"God, you fucking pussy," Clay sneered, and

Robin could see enough of his expression to read the fear there, a fear which Clay would not admit to under torture. He didn't want to go down into the darkness any more than Robin did, but he would, if only to prove how tough he was.

Suddenly Robin was furious. "Come on!" he shouted, his hands balling into fists. "You're just as scared as me! Can you just admit it? Can you just stop acting so fucking cool and manly all the time? You're not cool, you're just being a fucking asshole!"

His anger drained away as abruptly as it had welled up. All at once, he was terrified Clay would kick the shit out of him. There was certainly a look on his face like he might.

But in the end, all Clay did was turn away and say, in a cold, flat voice, "Fuck you. You can leave. Go wait up on deck if you're gonna be such a little bitch."

He put his foot through the hatch and set it on the top rung of the ladder.

Robin stood unmoving. His anger had burnt out like a flashbulb, leaving him tired and cold and scared and sad. He watched Clayton descend into the hold, heard the splash as his feet hit the water. He knew how this would shake out: come Monday, when Clay was in a better but no less spiteful mood, he'd spread the story of this night about. Everyone would know how the two of them had come out here to explore the shipwreck, but then Robin had pussied out, because he was scared of ghosts or water or just because he was a pussy and that was what pussies did.

Robin set his jaw. No. Fuck Clay. He wasn't gonna let that asshole mock him to anyone who would listen. He was gonna go down there after him. Maybe kick his ass while he was at it. Fuck him.

He took one step towards the hatch—and then he felt it again, the thing he'd felt when he touched the wall, now coming up through the soles of his shoes: that bone-deep thrum, like the slow turning of some colossal engine. It rattled in his ribs, and even as he opened his mouth, it grew into noise, a rising groan, a shriek. "Clay!" he screamed.

The floor bucked underneath him, and he tumbled through the hatch.

The next thing he knew, he was slumped uncomfortably against the ladder. His pants were soaked through with cold water, but his face was warm. Clayton was standing over him and saying, "Christ. Jesus Christ. Can you hear me? Are you okay, dude?"

Robin gingerly touched his fingers to the warmth on his face, then inspected them by the light of Clay's flashlight. They were red with blood. A rusty sob issued from his lips. The noise surprised him. "I wanna leave," he mumbled.

"Yeah, we're leaving, we're gonna leave." Clay angled his flashlight upwards, and Robin felt a stab of dull horror as he saw that the hatch at the top of the ladder was now closed. It must've fallen shut after he fell through it, when the yacht—

"It moved," he moaned. "The wreck. It's coming loose."

"Yeah. We're leaving. Hang on. Just—" Clay pressed his flashlight into Robin's hands, then climbed the ladder. Robin's own flashlight was nowhere to be seen. Lying on the floor of the galley above, probably. He sat in the icy water, aiming the light at the top of the ladder, where Clayton was shoving his shoulder against the hatch.

It didn't budge. It must have jammed when it closed.

They were trapped.

With a sharp pant of breath, Clay gave up. He hopped off the ladder, his boots splashing freezing water onto Robin's leg, and snatched the flashlight out of Robin's unresisting hand. He swept its beam across the hold in search of some other way out.

The wreck was still thrumming, still throbbing. It was not like an engine after all. It was too… organic. Somehow, awfully, alive.

Clay stopped. He whispered, "What the fuck?"

Robin struggled to his feet, using the ladder for support. He palmed blood out of his eyes and watched as Clay slowly approached one side of the hold, where the lurching of the wreck had opened the hull's inner layer of planking like a ribcage. Clay's face was perfectly blank, save for a tiny furrow of confusion between his brows. He reached out with his free hand, grabbed one of the wooden ribs, and wrenched the opening wider.

The wreck shuddered around them, and in the beam of the flashlight Robin caught a glimpse of the inside of the hull, a greasy shine like guts.

Then the wreck heaved again, even more violently, screaming as it tore free of the reef. It pitched to one side, and Robin lost his balance and tumbled down on top of Clay. He flailed blindly, trying to get off him, trying to stand even as the wreck canted sickeningly around them. The flashlight had gone out. He heard screaming, and recognized the voice as his own.

"It's not unfair," Clay had said about lobster fishing that one time, sneering the way he did whenever Robin said anything even remotely philosophical. "It's natural. Lots of animals do it. Like spiders, or those plants that eat bugs."

They'd been having this conversation on the beach, where they had gone to smoke. Clay had been skipping stones out across the gray water, one after another, watching them sink with faraway eyes.

"It's not just humans who use traps."

UNDONE
Max Turner

Tommy screamed.

He sank back into the waves as though the sand had given out beneath his feet. Unable to stand, the pain was beyond excruciating when he felt his ankle give way, felt it crunch. It was as if the plate just wasn't there any more, like his surgery had never happened.

It had melted away in the waves. Become undone.

"No!" Tommy cried out. This time in desperation as he saw Oliver on the shore. His vision blurred with the pain, but he could see his boyfriend running towards him and crashing into the surf. Tommy's protests went unheard, and Oliver began wading towards him from where he'd been sitting on the beach, enjoying the last of the sun. Tommy watched as each of Oliver's steps became visibly more difficult.

Tommy held up his hand to stop him, to wave him away.

"No, Oliver! Please, get out. Go back!" Tommy begged through his own pain.

"Tommy, I've got you," Oliver called out as he pushed forward. The agony on his face grew more intense the closer he drew, the further the sun went down and the deeper the water became.

Oliver clenched his jaw as the water turned black around them, a deep and unnatural colour that was more than the coming darkness of night. It was viscous, syrupy like oil, like blood.

"Oliver please," Tommy begged. "Leave me."

Oliver's eyes were full of determination as he struggled through the thick water and took hold of Tommy. With an arm around Tommy's waist, Oliver dragged him back to the shoreline one torturous step at a time until they were clear, and the black sludge slid from their skin, receding back into the waves.

They dropped to the wet sand with a grunt.

Tommy had understood his own pain very quickly. A flash of painful memories and the sensations in his leg had made him accurately aware of the sudden absence of the metal that had become part of his body over a decade ago, after his accident.

"Oliver—" Tommy started, terrified of what it would have done to his boyfriend. What if it had done the same to him? Undone his surgery. . .

Oliver had turned his back to him and was heaving his breaths, not hyperventilating but very far from calm. He was trembling and Tommy wanted to reach out to him, but something held him back.

He could see the stretch of Oliver's shirt, the curve when he turned slightly.

"Are you alright?" Tommy asked quietly, knowing the words were meaningless.

When Oliver didn't reply, Tommy moved closer.

"Does it hurt?" Tommy forced the words out through his own pain, emotional now as well as physical.

He was relieved at least when Oliver shook his head.

"Not. . .not physically."

"Fuck," Tommy muttered under his breath. "What the hell is happening?"

Tommy shook his head, trying to understand the last few minutes and what had happened to them. He was terrified and all he knew for sure was that his ankle surgery and Oliver's top surgery had both been undone.

Twelve hours earlier they had arrived at this tropical beach resort, and even then, they had both known something was off. The vibe in the place had been uncomfortable, but they had planned this break for so long and the horror of what was happening was beyond all imagining.

As soon as Oliver's top surgery scars had healed, Tommy had looked for a nice, secluded place for their vacation. This ridiculously cheap hotel, small with its own private beach, seemed perfect. The deal was done when Tommy read up on the area and the local legends of sea gods and monsters, the sort of stuff Oliver loved reading about.

He had booked it because he knew how much Oliver loved the beach. How much he longed to finally have a beach vacation without wearing layers or a binder. A vacation where he could now be free to completely enjoy himself. He had booked it because he wanted to see Oliver's face light up when they visited local sites and learned more about the local legends of human sacrifices to control the god of this sea.

In truth, they had both been prepared for it not being a queer friendly place, for them to have to curb their affections. That was often standard, and Tommy had dismissed the strangeness of the hotel staff for this reason.

But now this? Whatever it was.

Tommy's hand was shaking as he reached out to touch Oliver's shoulder. When Oliver flinched away, Tommy felt a deep pain wrench in his chest.

"I can't," Oliver murmured. "I can't fall apart. Need to be strong."

Tommy felt his heart breaking, wishing he could take away the pain Oliver was experiencing, knowing those same words had been his mantra until he began to 'pass'.

"Oliver—" Tommy started, wanting to comfort him, but Oliver cut him off.

"I'm not going to be beaten by this. I don't put up with all the fucking hateful nonsense day in, day out, for this to happen." Sweet, gentle Oliver growled the words.

When Oliver turned to him, Tommy was struck dumb by the rage in his boyfriend's eyes. They had been together over five years, and he had never seen this in Oliver before. He had held Oliver when he cried, agreed with him when he ranted, but he had never seen something so dark and terrifying. Like something within him had finally snapped.

"One day, someone was going to push me too far." Oliver muttered the words as he got to his feet, his jaw tight and high. Tommy knew he was trying not to look down, trying not to see what the strange water had done to him.

After a moment, Oliver reached down to pull Tommy up, but he shook his head.

"You should leave me, I can't walk. This ankle...After the accident and the surgery, it took me months to walk again. And now the plate has gone."

He didn't dare look down at his ankle either. Not needing the visual on the mangled mess he knew was there. He had once thought it would stop him from ever walking again, but the doctors managed to rebuild. The thought made his throat ache.

"I'm not leaving you," Oliver growled then looked around, as though trying to find something that might help them, but there was nothing. Nothing but a mile of fine, white sand, barely visible in the last light of the setting sun.

"Oliver, our bag!" Tommy pointed to the beach bag they had brought with them earlier, sitting just a little further up from the water.

It seemed so mundane now. Part of a day that had been normal, until it hadn't been.

Oliver grabbed it and emptied it out onto the sand. His Kindle, a beach towel, two bottles of water and some sun cream. Both of their phones were there, Tommy's out of battery and no signal on Oliver's.

Tommy held up Oliver's phone, trying to see if he could get any reception.

"A bar, no. It's gone." Tommy tried to quell his panic. Who would they call? What was the emergency services number here? They should get back to the hotel for help, but the shiver down his spine told Tommy that would be a mistake.

When he looked back at Oliver, he was just sitting there quietly, both bottles of water in his hands.

He had never cared how Oliver looked, he loved him regardless and never thought him any less of a man before top surgery. But to see his wet shirt with medium sized breasts free beneath, not even bound, was jarring. Tommy felt a pain deep in his gut, knowing how much this was hurting Oliver and how little he could do to help him.

Tommy wanted to tell him it would be okay. They would get out of this, fix this. *It wasn't forever.* The same words Tommy had used to keep him sane during the three years it had taken to save the money for the surgery.

He only fought through that lump in his throat when Oliver stood abruptly.

"Oliver?"

"Keep trying to get a signal. I'll come back for you, I promise."

After a moment, Oliver dropped in front of Tommy and kissed him, a rough and urgent kiss as he held him by the back of the neck. It was a distorted echo of the kiss they had shared on this beach earlier, rolling in the sand and laughing whilst the sun was still high in the afternoon sky.

Oliver pulled away and stood, taking the two bottles and stalking off.

Tommy kept looking at the phone, taking only a few minutes of seeing no bars before he decided it was pointless. As darkness descended, the beach felt vast and wrong. He felt compelled to try and reach Oliver.

Putting the phone in his pocket, Tommy tried to stand, stifling a cry of pain.

He composed himself, trying to work out the

best way to get across the sand without putting weight on through his ankle.

When he heard the first scream, Tommy started crawling, dragging himself towards the hotel. His ankle, twisted and mangled, now looked as though it had healed in an instant in that malformed shape before the doctors had worked on him.

It was agony, but desperation spurred him on.

"Oliver!"

The hotel drew closer, sitting there perfectly on the edge of the beach. Bright white walls lit up by the rising half-moon, but unmistakable red in the doorway.

Red everywhere.

"Oliver!" Tommy ached as he continued to drag himself forward. The effort was incredible, the sand making it difficult to get any real purchase and the pain increasingly slowing him down in painfully sharp increments.

There was another scream as he finally reached the doorway, this time clearly feminine. Tommy had only just registered it when a woman ran past him and out onto the beach.

He recognised her from earlier that day, the receptionist who had checked them in.

Still screaming, she looked behind her, resulting in her tripping in the sand and falling to the ground.

Tommy heard the crunching of the plastic bottle before he saw Oliver coming out of the hotel after her. He stalked straight past him, completely focused on the woman.

Tommy managed to pull himself up against

the door frame of the grand front doors of the hotel as he watched the scene unfold.

"Oliver, what's happening?"

In Oliver's hand was one of the water bottles, uncapped and half full of thick, black water. He stood over the woman, illuminated by the harsh artificial light thrown out through the open doors.

Oliver didn't respond to Tommy, instead he emptied the bottle over her, dousing her with the water, though it might as well have been acid. She shrieked and coiled in on herself, her body disintegrating into pus and blood in places and ageing in others so that it shrivelled to almost nothing until her screams ceased.

Within seconds there was nothing but a strange husk in a pool of dark blood quickly soaking into the sand.

"Ol-Oliver?" Tommy was shaking as Oliver turned; there was more blood all over him, smeared on his face, his hands. All over the bottle.

"Lucky guess," Oliver said as though that explained everything. He threw the almost empty bottle down onto the desiccated remains of the receptionist before slowly walking back to Tommy.

Oliver leaned against the other side of the door jamb as Tommy looked inside the hotel.

The reception desk was covered in blood, the office door behind it was open, a bloody handprint running down it. A mixture of blood and viscera had been walked all over the lobby. And presiding over it all stood the statue that dominated the centre of the space.

"What happened?" Tommy asked through his

tears.

"The water, I filled it from the beach. I thought it would do what it did to us. Undo surgeries, hurt them. I hadn't expected this. But then after the first one, they tried to... I had to. All of them. Do you understand?" Oliver looked at him with determination and yes, Tommy did understand.

"Sometimes you can only be pushed so far before you fight back," Tommy said quietly, and Oliver nodded.

The silence that fell over them was broken by a ping in Tommy's pocket. He pulled out the phone and found a social media alert had popped up, almost a full signal.

"We have a signal. Who do we call? The police?"

"How do we explain this?" Oliver gestured to his chest, to the bodies.

"I don't know. What do we do now?" Tommy asked, his mind reeling.

When he looked back at Oliver, he realised his boyfriend was gazing back into the lobby, at that huge statue that had given them the creeps when they arrived.

Some sort of sea god. Or monster.

At the same moment, they realised it was calling to them.

Twelve Hours Earlier

Despite their suitcase, Tommy insisted they get dropped at the beachfront path and walk down to what was considered the front entrance of the hotel, rather than the back entrance that sat on the coast road.

"Where did you find this place anyway?" Oliver asked, shaking his head and chuckling as he watched Tommy struggle with their case along the sand covered path.

"I honestly can't remember, it was a while ago now. Maybe a Facebook ad? The price is fantastic. I can't believe it costs so little when the hotel has this private beach, everything is onsite. It's just—"

"Perfect," Oliver completed the sentence, but Tommy didn't miss the cocked brow and the slight derision in his tone. Not so much a pessimist, Oliver was always ready with a criticism. He was what Tommy liked to call a delightful asshole.

"And the reviews were good?" Oliver asked, leadingly.

"They were great." Tommy replied, poking Oliver gently in the ribs. "Stop being a dick."

"To you? Never." Oliver grinned at him, and Tommy rolled his eyes.

"Being hypercritical is going to become your defining trait," Tommy mused as they got to the front of the hotel.

In an equally light tone, Oliver replied, "I'm not hypercritical, I'm wary."

Tommy wasn't going to argue with that. Being trans, Oliver had a lot to be wary of. It had been an eye opener even to Tommy, who had experienced his own share of discrimination over the years. He knew how tiring it was and longed for a day when Oliver didn't need to be on his guard all the time.

As they approached the double doors, a concierge opened them into the lavish lobby.

"Gentleman, so good to see you."

Before they could even cross the threshold from the beach into the lobby, both of their gazes were drawn to the strange and slightly menacing statue in the centre of the room. Despite a fish-like tail, it looked more like a gargoyle than a merman. His face held a distorted smile that initially seemed like the poor workmanship of the sculptor but, on second glance, perhaps was purposeful.

Standing next to the statue were three other members of staff, apparently there to greet them. With their insincere smiles, there was something even Tommy found creepy about them and knew immediately Oliver would have something to say.

"You are our only guests this weekend, so we are delighted to be able to give you our full attention." The concierge spoke warmly but a warmth that seemed only surface deep. Like the smile that didn't reach his eyes. "It's been so long since we've had such flamboyant guests," the concierge continued with a cutting tone that set Tommy on edge. He could feel Oliver tense up next to him.

It was mid-afternoon now, and they were both jetlagged, so Tommy resolved that they would enjoy the beach into the evening and worry about it later. If it turned out the place was a complete wash out, then he'd find another hotel for them up in the town.

Twelve Years Later

Tommy and Oliver strolled along the beach hand in hand. They could no longer swim in the water here; that was part of the deal they had made that night. But it was beautiful, nonetheless.

They took a slow pace, Tommy walked with a slight limp – an ill effect that remained of their first night in this place. The surgery he had needed after that night wasn't as successful as when he'd originally had the plate put in. There was still a little pain, but nothing he couldn't cope with. Walking on sand would always be difficult, but it was such a glorious vista it was hard to resist.

The contemplative quiet was abruptly disrupted by the boisterous noises of a group coming down the beach path towards the hotel entrance.

Both Tommy and Oliver looked back at the four men making their way along the sand covered path to the entrance. They continued to hold hands as they started to make their way back to welcome them. Then their eyes met and one of the men sneered.

"Fuck John. You didn't tell me there would be fags here." He spat the words, clearly with the intent of having them overheard. Grumbling amongst themselves, the men ambled in through the open doors and into the lobby.

Oliver turned to Tommy with a pleasant smile.

"Darling, it looks like our new guests have arrived."

"Perhaps they'd like an evening swim." Oliver's reply was immediate and cold.

There was that familiar glint in Oliver's eyes, a hint of rage beneath something more calculated. Dark and powerful, just like the beloved statue that loomed over them all.

SWALLOW THE OCEAN
Daphne Fama

Angela knew the ocean intimately. Better than she knew herself. She knew the ocean was beautiful at a distance, terrifying at its medium, but up close there was one thing no one ever wanted to admit: it reeks. And there was no escaping that smell. The brine works its way into your mouth and twists your tongue with its acrid bitterness.

That stench claws its way into your throat. It convinces you that you enjoy the taste of its ugliness. And that's to say nothing of the ever present, perpetual touch of death laced within that smell. The ocean is so many multi-faceted things, but more than anything else, it is a charnel house. A place where things are born only to die, and to die in great numbers. The carcasses, large and small, that gather where sea meets sand, are only a fraction of the death held within those black waters. They are mottled, swollen, and docile, tangled in the lank brown of kelp. Primarily, these corpses are fish, but not always.

The ocean reek entwined itself around Angela as it did every day. She sucked in the salt air and the electric taste of the approaching storm, letting it swell her chest. The fetid air found a place in her heart next to the loneliness that hurt so much it threatened to crack her ribs.

These past few months, there was something new to the stench, something subtle, just beneath the surface. It was the smell of her mother's skin, baked in the morning sun, unmistakable. And yet it mingled now with the ocean's reek of death.

Angela's fraying Styrofoam sandals slapped against the bottom of her heels as she walked down the battered pier. Splinters tried to stab at her through the soles, into her callused feet. The sun crawled up over the mountains at her back, burning away the light mist that wreathed Carigara. But the twilight kept the ocean black, and most of the anglers were already out to sea, their long boats bobbing in the waves, filled with leather-skin old men and young, lean boys. They weren't much older than her. Maybe thirteen, fourteen. Usually, they were far out to sea, but they seemed to gravitate towards the pier. And despite the dimness of the new day, she could almost see the glint in their eyes, watching her.

If her mother was still here, she and her mother would be in a boat too, drifting in the waves. They'd sit together wreathed in the last vestiges of the night, the ocean splashing up at them. She'd watch her mother lean over the side of their old, reliable boat. She'd watch her mother narrow her eyes at the water, as if she could see precisely where all the ocean's morsels hid.

Angela would wait for her mother's call, a quick gesture of the hand. And once she saw it, she'd dive into the water like a seal at her tamer's command. She felt the most whole when her body cut through the waves, when the water dug into her short, cropped hair. Angela would push herself as far as her body could go, until her lungs burned and ached in her chest. Until her hands felt the soft, unmistakable tenderness of the ocean floor's flesh, and her callused fingertips butted against the hard rock. In the crevices of these sharp stones her hands would search, until finally she hit the hard, sleek shell of a snail.

If she was quick enough, she'd be able to wrest the snail from its nook before it could pull itself tight against a rock. But most times she didn't. Instead, she'd slink back to the surface and stare into her mother's waiting eyes. Eyes that knew even before Angela broke the surface whether she'd succeeded or not.

"You have to swallow the ocean before you learn all its secrets. You're afraid of what's in it, so it gives you nothing," her mother drawled in her thick Bisyan accent, a mantra that dripped patience and disappointment in equal measure. Then she'd strip off her thin jacket and dive beneath the waves. Her mother would shoot through the ocean like an arrow, sinking hard and fast as if she belonged in the black waters. She'd stay under for so long that Angela would sometimes wonder if she'd ever come back.

Precisely when Angela would begin to worry, when she'd begin to entertain thoughts that she might never see her mother again, her mother would emerge in the water beside her. Her sun-leathered face gleaming in the breaking dawn, her dark eyes flashing with triumph as she hefted the sea snail onto the boat. The beautifully curled triton's trumpet, the clawed edges of the giant spider conch. Anything smaller was a waste of her mother's time.

She and her mother would do this again and

again, until there was a small treasure trove between them. The only time the ocean doesn't smell is when it's still alive. When the fish are caught fresh.

The other anglers hated her mother and, by extension, Angela. No one could dive as well as her mother. No one had her uncanny sense for finding the dark, hidden nooks the snails found sanctuary in. A single snail could fetch more money than a dozen fish. So succulent was its flesh when cooked well, so savory and rich. Fish could fill a man's stomach, but the white flesh of a snail could make you feel alive.

Now, though, Angela was alone. Her mother had vanished one day, when Angela had been too lazy to join her mother on the waves. Her boat floated back to shore, empty.

No one saw anything. No one knew where she'd gone.

That's what they said, though Angela knew that there were at least a dozen other set of eyes on the ocean when her mother vanished.

Angela spent weeks searching for her, walking the shorelines, cutting her feet on the barnacle-riddled rocks surrounding the village. She searched the mangroves near the river that opened into the sea, in case her mother had tangled herself in their roots, finding a home somewhere between land and sea. But she found nothing, and no one seemed to care. The anglers seemed to plump and glow in her mother's absence, and she hated the way they swept into the wet market, baskets full of fish and snails a fraction of the size her mother would have caught.

She knew in the darkest recesses of her pumping heart that her mother didn't abandon her.

Her mother loved her, almost as she loved the ocean. She would have never left either of them.

But in her mother's absence, Angela's ribs pressed through her skin. Her cheek bones were sharp, and her hair lost some of its gloss. She couldn't dive like her mother, and the pantry was stocked with spiderwebs and dust. The only thing of value she had left was her mother's old boat. She chewed on her sun-chapped lips and watched as a fisherman at the end of the pier unspooled the rope docking her mother's boat, as if it was already his. As if this whole conversation was nothing but a formality, a token of generosity from him to her. She sized him up, the way her mother would the sea before a storm. He'd become soft in the months since her mother's passing. But when he smiled at her, his grin was a rotted black.

"Shame about your mother, Angela. But one thousand pesos is the best I can do."

"A thousand?" Angela echoed, her mouth twisting. "You're practically stealing from me. My mother bought that boat for twenty thousand."

He scoffed. "Sure, ten years ago. But now it's old, isn't it? And cursed at that. No one wants the boat of a dead woman, do they?" He glanced towards the ocean, where the boats of the other anglers bobbed on their sea, watching the exchange with drawn, expressionless faces.

"No one else will buy this boat but me. So, you might as well take what you can get." He extended the wrinkled and wet knot of one-hundred-peso bills towards her, his other hand intertwined with the boat's leash, as if it was already his.

Angela's blood burned to see his hands on it,

and tears threatened to well at the corner of her eyes. She bit them back and set her jaw.

"Then no. I can't sell it to you."

He blinked, and his abscessed smile flattened. "This is the best deal you're going to get, girl. You're lucky I'm doing any business with you at all. No one else here would. Most people told me to take the boat straight out, once it hit the shores empty. But I know you worked hard, and I know it's hard to lose your parents. So, I'm doing this as a favor. Take the money."

"No," she repeated, her hands turning to fists at her side. She'd made the decision. She'd starve before she let her mother's boat go to him. She'd cast it out to sea, with her body still in it, and let the ocean take both of them.

The fisherman spat and shoved the bills into his pocket. His gaze trailed off towards the black waters beside them, his expression somber. "That's a shame. But maybe it's all for the best. It's better to go fast than slow. And you'd go real slow, out here all by yourself."

She stared at him, not quite comprehending what he meant. But he turned to her, dropping the rope of the boat, and grabbed her by the waist. She was a paltry ninety pounds, and he hefted her with a sinewy strength that shocked her into silence.

But as he dragged her towards the end of the pier, she screamed, her limbs thrashing.

"Help! Please, help," she shouted to the anglers, watching from their boats in a loose circle around the pier. They watched her as if she was mute. As if she was a fish, gasping for air, destined to be gutted.

Grunting, he tossed her off the pier and into the ocean. The water swirled around her, its waves pushed her down. But its cold touch was familiar, and her eyes flashed open, straining to see against the murk and shadow of the pier above.

The tall, wooden legs of the pier flanked her, covered in an army of barnacles. Fish gathered and circled around one of the pillars, ravenous and bold despite her presence. Their silver scales flashed in stark contrast to the darkened figure pressed against the pier's leg.

A woman, her clothes tattered, lay against the wood, kept just beneath the surface. Her black hair flowed like a halo around her head. When it swept away, Angela could see the voids which had once housed eyes.

The fish and crabs hadn't taken their time. They'd devoured the body in large swaths, peeling back its skin and burrowing into the meat, so countless holes gaped in the face and chest. The legs and arms were long gone, dropped somewhere below. The disfigured face, what was left of it, was swollen by water, the tattered remains of flesh lifting from the bones beneath. But Angela knew the face of her mother, marred as it was by the ocean. How could she not know the face of her mother?

She stared, transfixed. Thick ropes bound her mother around her waist and throat. Perhaps the only thing still keeping her head atop her body. All those hours Angela spent searching, and her mother had always been here. Her body had drawn the fish, turning them fat, and the fishermen had prospered because of it.

Kicking upwards, Angela broke the surface and gasped for breath. Hot tears streamed down her face. The fisherman stared down at her from the pier. Their eyes met, and she recoiled at the poison in his dark eyes. She swam backwards on instinct, slipping further out to the sea.

"You can't come back to shore now," he called down to her, his voice nearly lost to the static buzzing in her brain. He shucked the shirt off his back and dived into the water, still athletic despite his age and newfound softness. Before Angela could react, he was on her, his callused thickened hands pushing her head beneath the surface.

Was this how he killed her?

She thought as he held her down, and the fear and panicked numbness that had gripped her turned to an electric heat. Her hands twitched with a life of their own, as if her anger had finally found form. She grabbed at him, scratching at his bare chest, even as he kept her under. Her hands found his neck. She dug her thumbs into his throat and a gush of air slid past his lips, bubbling into the water. He shoved her down again, hard, but she clung to him like the snails on the rock. Her skeletal legs wrapped around his chest, and she dug her hands in deeper.

With her weight anchored to him, they sank, twirling in a death dance. But she refused to let go of his throat. She dug her nails into the skin and pressed her thumbs as deep as they could go. His hands tore at her hair and punched at her face. Scarlet blossomed around them. Someone was bleeding, but she wasn't sure who. Her body was awash with the cold of the ocean, her blood burned beneath her skin.

He tore a chunk of her hair out, sending the soft, wispy tendrils into a crown around his flailing fist. Still, she didn't relent. Another handful of seconds passed. His blows grew weaker, turned almost pleading as they pushed at her body, trying to pry Angela off him. He'd never been as good as her mother at diving, at living beneath the water. But Angela wasn't afraid of the ocean, wasn't afraid of her lungs exploding in her chest even as stars lit in front of her eyes, turning the bloodied waters into a scarlet Milky Way.

She pressed harder, with all her strength, and watched with bared teeth as the fisherman's lips turned slack and silver bubbles gushed between his rotted teeth. His last pocket of air. His jaundiced eyes stared through her, glassy and confused. His taut throat softened. Some part of it had given way, broken and irreparable. She unrooted her fingers from his neck, and his body drifted to the ocean floor, sending a soft cloud of silt up. His arms reached for her, for the pale circle of sun high above.

Angela's lungs burned in her chest; her heart pounded in her ears. She opened her mouth and let the ocean flood her throat. She swallowed it, so its bitterness churned in her stomach, and tilted her head to the surface. Beneath her mother's blackened gaze, she rose. The boats overhead crowded in, their shadows swirling like sharks.

osedax
Marisca Pichette

We felt you sinking
lungs drawing water like blood
        you made ripples in your flailing
& We heard.

We are waiting where you drift
onto sand that was never
a beach.
        your eyes We have no interest in
though you stare at the Others,
the Big Feeders who traverse
abyssal plains strewn with coral
bones.

We are courteous. We let the Big Feeders have you first,
unmake your face
leave remnants our smaller fellows gather
in translucent claws.

do you fear us?

We are patient.
        when the Big Feeders have freed your flesh
& swam, engorged, into the depths
We descend.

We make no shadows, here in the ever dark.
We need no light to find your hardest parts
& plant our roots.

do you feel naked, skin unbound,
muscles unspooled by lampreys
in the deep?

are you cold,
*   collapsed*
now all but white
has gone?

you are not lost. you are not nothing.

We see your barrenness as bounty.

We cover you now, reassemble the meat you lost
to larger mouths.
    our teeth are less
    than you can count
but our bites are strong.

We bore into you—a mat of ruby
reenacting your dear departed blood.
in our coming, you are connected
to orcas, greys, belugas.

In our coming, you are bound
to oceans unending.

In our coming, you are not
alone.

We have no borders, no territories we fear
to cross in our search
—this quest: taking what has fallen
trapped under crushing waves
& turning you at last into
        electricity.
the power to dwell in darkness
& never be lost.

in us, We bring you through
to the other side
of dying.

in us, We seek for you
another descended soul,
bubbles in their wake.

Let their bones light the way
& never lie forgotten
within all ocean's heart.

THE ODD-YSSEY
Davis Walden

A Grecian trireme shambled its way towards us out from the murky dark. Fog snared up around two painted eyes on its bow that glared across the waterline. The eyes dipped and vanished beneath the waves, only to reappear when the depths allowed. A black fiddlehead curl towered above the bow, like a headdress for those gorgon-like eyes. It sloshed water up against the loading dock, knocking into the walls of the narrow waterway. The fifteen years of Sisyphean journeys through treacherous waters had left it battered and scratched, the paint of a ship having been to Colchis and back.

    I shuddered. A nervous sweat built on the middle of my back and it didn't help that Tristen and I were still feeling the effects of the heat we had just escaped. It was a hot, crowded summer's day at Uncharted Worlds. We spent most of the day just trying to warm me up for this absolute nightmare of a ride.

    I knew that I'd be okay doing any of the roller coasters, so we rode those first. We swept through Jupiter's Storm in Galaxyland, The Snow Queen in Mysticland, and The Howler in Terrorland. Then, we leveled up to the dark rides with some animatronics hanging out in the open. Mysticland and Terrorland had the majority, so I braced myself. Morgana's

Wrath was the worst for me. It had a massive dragon at the end that lunged out at the car with a blaring truck horn. I screamed so bad Tristen practically had to smother me so I wouldn't scare the children.

With three lands down, we ventured into Ancientland. The park *darling*. This is what we'd prepared for. What I dreaded most. Ancientland was the adventure land for the archaeologically inclined. It's home to most of the park's water rides, including a river raft ride called Ruins of Atlantis and, Tristen's favorite, a Nordic log ride called Ragnarök.

Ragnarök was a fucking monstrosity. It's a dark ride that introduced you to animatronics of the Norse gods, Vikings, Valkyries, and, finally, Fenrir and Jörmungandr. As you're being chased by Fenrir's snarling shadow up the length of the hill leading up to the final drop, Jörmungandr opens his maw and tries to swallow you. Soaked to the bone, we got our photos at the booth. Tristen had on a wide smile and I was trapped in a horrified scream as went down the fifty foot drop.

"Whew! That was a close one!" Sylvie the seal, dressed in a Grecian tunic, said off in the distance to another ship's passengers. She waved her fin back and forth as she popped out from the water. "Be sure to watch your step when you get out of the boat! Let's go on another quest soon!"

A sign decorated with waves and coral-covered Ionic columns, sat on the other end of the wall, saying *The Odd-yssey*.

This was going to be our last stop.

Tristen slipped off his backpack and held it in his hands as he placed himself at the loading dock. I was still over by the attendant. "Are you ready?"

I nodded.

A group of teenagers laughed their way out of the boat, exiting out the other side. I envied how easy it was for them to ignore the danger. They were so blissfully unaware of what lurked in these dark waters, filled with hydraulic fluid and rotating gears. Eyes that blinked without a proper rhythm. Faces that turned a little too strongly from side to side.

The boat bobbled towards us. Those empty, droplet-covered seats beckoned us to be the next souls on their way through the Mediterranean Sea– or to Hades, because there was no way we would be leaving this ride alive.

It was our turn.

Tristen placed his hand on the small of my back. "I'm proud of you. I know this is a big step." He kissed me on the cheek and hopped into the boat.

"Are you ready to go on a quest?" the attendant, some college-aged kid dressed in an Ionic column-accented uniform, said in a droning monotone with a smile. He chimed through the over-rehearsed instructions to us as we got in and settled, but I didn't hear any of it. I was too busy noticing that we were alone. No one else was getting in the boat with us. "Be sure to keep your hands, arms, and legs inside the ship."

He pressed a button on the podium and the ride shook out of the loading dock.

But right before we sailed off into the darkness, I caught the end of a sentence from some woman in the line: "...they're brand new! So much more lifelike."

We dropped.

* * *

I yelped with the splash.

"You okay?" Tristen asked. I pulled myself closer up against him and buried my head into his shoulder.

"Yeah, yeah," I said. "It's just—"

"You can do this," Tristen said as glorious music began to swell. Lyrical lyres with a golden hum. "Because we. . ."

"W—we can do anything."

Tristen smiled as we came into the light and I was thankful to have a sun of my own. He was right. With him, we could do anything. *I* could do anything. I could sit down on a tracked boat on a dumb, stupid ride for kids and. . .and. . .I could see all of those monsters. All of those creatures I wasn't familiar with anymore because they've updated the ride. Oh God. What all did they change?

Our ship approached a seaside collection of islands with stone homes and marble temples running down along the cliffside. A herd of goats bleated as we passed by. I grimaced. The people in line were right. These weren't the same animatronics from the accident. These were new. They didn't jerk their heads back and forth, their eyes didn't blink unevenly. No, they looked real. Cartoonishly stylized, but a work of Pygmalion's come alive.

I tugged at Tristen's shirt and squirmed closer to him. "They've changed them out. They're different.

Tristen sat his fingers on my thigh and squeezed. "Hey, it's okay. You can do this."

Sylvie the Seal, speckled black and grey and white, popped her head out of the water.

"Ah, fuck!" I cried out. "Fuck, fuck, fucking shit, mother fucker."

The smallest hint of a smile crept across Tristen's lips as he tried to calm me down.

Sylvie's lightless, lifeless, black, inky eyes stared at us as she crept back down under into the depths.

Sylvie lunged out into the open on a platform. "Hello! I haven't seen you here in Ithaca before. Are you new here? I'm Sylvie! Nice to meet you. I'm actually just about to hear my prophecy. Do you want to join me? I really hope the gods have something good in store for me!"

We veered away from the sunshine and the sea, drifting off to the entrance of a temple with snakes disguised in its decorative motifs. The tall void of an entrance yawned for us, smoke escaping from what lurked inside.

"This way!" Sylvie said.

* * *

The boat wobbled in through a narrow waterway. We cut past torches and cracks in the stone that let out jets of smoke and bright orange light. This part truly sucked. It sucked when I was a kid and it sucked now. The carved relief of a gorgon's snake-covered head screamed in silence as its eyes glowed green and gas spewed out from its unseen throat.

"*What lurks beyond, lurks just inside,*
Creeping forth from before our time," a voice said from afar.

"*Creatures, monsters, wait in the tide.*"

Sylvie backed away. "Monsters?"

Monsters waiting in the tide. They weren't waiting for Sylvie, though. They were waiting for me. I needed to get out of here. I needed to leave now. While there was still a chance.

A woman in a loose, tattered purple chiton was clawing at the walls. The movements... they were too smooth. They were so, so, so smooth. Her spindly fingers crept up and down the stones, picking at something only she could see. The woman whirled around, eyes glowing bright green. Sylvie gasped.

"*You and strangers must go fix the crime,*
Else we shall never see the summertime."

"Never see summer? What do you mean?" Sylvie exclaimed. "What crime? What am I supposed to do? I don't understand!"

The temple rumbled, gases screamed, and the earth began to roar.

"*Go!*" the priestess wailed.
"*The threads of fate are pulling,*
Just like the sea, the currents, rolling."

We rounded the corner as smoke engulfed the priestess.

"Wait! No! Come back!" Sylvie cried. "I don't know what to do!"

* * *

The temple exited out into a frozen sea basked in darkness. Ice clamored out across the landscape. The sounds of an intense blizzard filled up the room.

"Oh gods," Sylvie said. "What happened? It's so cold!"

Sylvie vanished behind a rock with a splash. Then, out from the waves, Sylvie popped up right next to me.

I screamed and huddled up against Tristen. "That's new! That's not how it was!"

Tristen shushed me as Sylvie said, "I just heard! The reins of Apollo's chariot are gone! The sun can't rise without them!"

"I have to get out of here," I said. "I need to leave."

I tried to sit up, but Tristen held me down. "You can't just *leave*. There's nowhere for you to go!"

There was a ledge not too far from us. All I needed was for the boat to move closer to it.

"*Please,* Tristen. I can get kicked out. Please just let me get kicked out."

"No, no! It's not safe. Just stay here and close your eyes if you need to, okay?"

"We just need to follow the currents!" Sylvie exclaimed. She dived back below.

I settled back down. "Fuck. I'm sorry. I'm sorry. I'm just—"

"Hey, hey, no, don't be sorry. You're fine. You're going to be fine."

"God. Fuck." We weren't even in the room where I fell in as a kid yet. We were just at the beginning and I was scared of a stupid cartoon seal. "I'm sorry."

Tristen kissed me. "Next room's coming up, are you okay?"

I readjusted in the seat and rubbed my hands across my face. "Yeah, yeah. I'm fine. I'm okay." I would have slapped myself for good measure, but I think that'd worry Tristen even more. He eyed me, cautiously, with that tight-lipped thing he does when he's concerned, and went back to taking in the world around us as we sank towards the next room through a frozen crevice.

The water tugged at the ship as we sloped down the drop and landed with a thud. The boat smacked the rubber sides and slobbered ahead through the rocks. Sylvie poked her head out through the rocks. She was wearing a bronze Greek helmet and leather armor with a red cape.

"I can swim through here safely, but you're going to have to watch out! This way! Over here!" Sylvie said, pointing at the rivulet going right, with a sign reading, "*Charybdis*." "The whirlpool's— Wait! Where are you going?"

The ship steered left.

"No! Don't! Come back! Scylla is that way!" Sylvie said, getting farther and farther away from us.

I slammed a hand down on Tristen's arm.

"This where it happened?" Tristen whispered.

I nodded so hard my head felt like it could have snapped off at the top.

"Okay," Tristen said. "You've done so good so far. If you want to close your eyes through this part, I get it."

I immediately buried myself into his arms and shut my eyes tight. I'd relived this scene so many times: the boat traverses past a string of rocks with heavy splashes and sprays, waterfalls that soak you wet, and, finally, the ship gets stuck. It gets lodged in the rocks. The waves crash around as hissing fills the air.

I could hear her coming for us. Scylla, the hydraulic hydra, and her many heads peeked out from caves in the cliffs and up from the water. Her yellow eyes glowed bright in the darkness. She blew smoke out of her nostrils in loud bursts and hissed screeching water jets at the boat.

"I've got you!" Sylvie cried as she dislodged the boat. "I'll fend her off!"

The music soared as Scylla roared, rising up into a crescendo as Sylvie raised her sword. We were so close to being free.

We shuddered forward then shuffled back. Then we stopped.

The music looped back around to the ominous start.

Tristen's breath caught in his throat. "We just stopped for a second. Don't–"

I sat up and looked around.

A reptilian head of Scylla burst out from the water and up next to my face. Scylla's purply-brown-green scales glistened as droplets of water trickled down and through the grooves of its renovated skin. Its new, fully realized animatronic face lunged forward.

I scrambled for purchase and crawled over onto Tristen's lap. "Oh God! No! No!"

Scylla's eyes glowed bright yellow and she screamed. A second head slashed out from the rocks to my left and gnashed the spitty teeth in its browning gums. It hissed out a jet of bright green gas.

"Sam, stop!" Tristen said, trying to push me down and cover my eyes, but I was way out of his reach and onto the back bench of the boat.

A third head was already there, next to the track behind us. It reared back, mouth closed, then jumped forward.

"*I remember you*," the Scylla head wheezed. "*Sammy.*"

"No! You don't know me!"

Tristen stood up and hopped into the back with me. "Sam! Sam! Calm down. I'm right here."

I fell back and looked around for a way out. This couldn't be it. There had to be a way out of here.

Sylvie's black eyes sprang out from the water. "I've got you!" Sylvie screamed. "I've got you now!"

I leaped out of the boat and fell straight into the water. I felt the track beneath my feet and pulled myself to a ledge. I was so much taller than I was back then when it happened – when I fell beneath where Scylla's head rested and waited underwater. I pulled myself up onto a ledge and ran down the cliffside, back the way we came. I didn't even look back as Tristen called my name.

I squeezed past the crack in the wall where we'd come through, edging myself along the ledge and through the water. There was another boat there. I stared at the confused batch of tourists before clamoring past them towards a path leading away from the river. It was the path Sylvie originally wanted you to go down, the one pointing towards Charybdis. It must have been an access tunnel for emergencies and maintenance. And this was an emergency.

Sylvie turned around and snagged my pants on her helmet. "Sammy. Come back! Scylla is that way!"

"No! Please!"

I wrenched myself free, bending Sylvie's helmet, and darted down the corridor.

"No! Don't! Come back! Scylla is that way!" Sylvie said as I disappeared into the next room.

The maintenance tunnel was strange. There weren't any lights blaring down the hallway, but I blamed myself; I wasn't supposed to be back here. Thing is, though, there were no pipes, no concrete floors, no handrails, heck, even the river from the ride flowed alongside me. It was as if the park knew to design an exit tunnel that was just as immersive as the ride itself. I wouldn't know what most tunnels looked like here. Who would? They were only ever used for emergencies, and ride disembarkment hardly ever happened. Then again, where were the handrails? Why were the stones uneven? I ran my hand along the wall to guide myself and discovered it *was* real stone. Moist and cold stone with smoothed over, weathered edges like it had been exposed to decades of watery molding. Whatever magics the theme park had used to create this place actually managed to calm me down some. It was cold and quiet, and a breeze wafted through the hall.

A loud splash echoed from where I came.

"I've got you!" Sylvie sing-songed. Her discordant notes bounced around with every one of her splashes.

I sprinted in a mad dash to nowhere. Keeping my hand on the wall, I guided myself down the hall, but it should have ended by now! There were no doors out, no sign of a life outside of the ride. Then I saw it. An exit sign glowing bright red down the way. Sylvie splished and splashed through the river, reciting nothing more than her lines from the ride every time she came up for air. She was so much faster than I was, so much more ready.

I slammed myself into the push bar and closed the door shut behind me.

Seagulls squawked as waves slapped against rocky outcroppings. Their spray sizzled in the ocean air and coated me wet.

I let go of the door and gaped. An ocean, one far unfamiliar to me, stormy and cold, sat before me. Rocks horned their way out of the waves like teeth in a circle and, behind that, a stretch of rocks stuck out of the sea like a canyon. One massive cut separated two towers of stone that stretched on for hundreds of miles. I stood on nothing more than two feet worth of outcropping. I yelped and backed up to the door, fingering for the handle. There wasn't one.

The door pushed forward and I shoved all of my weight back. A mighty thwack moved the door out a few more inches and I struggled for footing on the precipice. My sneakers scratched against the edge and caused splinters of rocks to fall into the ocean below.

"Wait! No! Come back!" Sylvie said. The whirs of her machinery sounded as she readied another shove. One more and I'd be gone.

"Please, no! No!"

"Come back!" Sylvie said, pushing on.

"PLEASE!" I cried out, scratching at the side of the door to see if I could grab the handle from the inside. "Leave me alone!"

"No!" Sylvie said. The hydraulics in her system roared and she pushed me forward.

I slipped my fingers out across the bar as I fell over the abyss. Sylvie stared at me with her dark eyes and, for the smallest moment, it looked as if she were actually concerned about me. Sylvie swiped for a fistful of shirt and missed as I swung out over the sea.

"Come back!" Sylvie said, her eyes blinking at me. She motioned at me with her hands to return to the cliff. To her. To what I could only, for an instant from instinct, describe as safety.

The door slapped against the cliff and my fingers twisted off of the bar.

I fell into the water below with a scream.

* * *

The water was colder than anything I had ever experienced. It jolted every pore of my body awake, then into fiery flares of pain. I reeled, swimming up for the surface, and came up into waves slapping me up against the rocks. I screeched as my body was scraped against the igneous holes and barnacles, tugged back, and slammed again. I got sucked back out into the water, hit by waves far too large that dragged me under and tumbling in the water.

I managed to scream my way up to the surface but found the current too strong to even paddle my way afloat. I turned around and saw the currents pulling the waves all around me into a tight coil. The vortex opened into a growing hole in the middle as many pointed rocks rose up from the sea below. Then I realized. They weren't rocks. They were teeth belonging to something far too large for me to even comprehend. What could even be this big? What sort of creature feasted on the sea like this?

I scurried for one of the teeth. They were smooth and round, but if I could just throw myself on it, then maybe I'd be spared becoming supper. I inched my way over as the currents pulled at every fiber of my being and swept straight past it into the whirling spiral.

Something wrapped around my waist and I looked down. It was a thick metal wire that tapered off at the end. The end of it crept up along my torso and licked at my head and neck and tickled loosely at the air. Then it pulled me under with such force I thought my waist was going to snap off.

The pressure lifted and I floated back up to the surface. I gasped and looked around. The wire was still wrapped around me but cleaved off at the end. Electric wires poked out as oil leaked, turning the ocean a brownish-black.

Sylvie surfaced and I screamed. She held her sword aloft. "I've got you! I'll fend her off!"

Two wires wrapped themselves around Sylvie's neck and arm, hoisting her up into the air.

One of the tentacles shifted its way down onto Sylvie's leg and the two wires – no, tentacles–tugged.

"Monsters?" Sylvie screamed. "Monsters? No!"

The tentacles crunched down Sylvie's armor as she screamed, the fake bronze and leather crumbling and cracking beneath the muscle's force. The metal of Sylvie's robotic skin pierced through the speckles of her false fur, yanking the fabric into awkward angles. The pressure gave way and Sylvie was torn in half. Her wires and oil and insides dropped down into the water along with her arm and sword. Sylvie's lifeless head and the armature connected inside, a messy tangle of metal like a spine, were whipped through the air and thrown tens of yards away. The bottom half of Sylvie's body dropped like it was nothing. It plopped into the ocean as I got sucked back under again by a current far stronger than the rest.

I spun through frigid water screaming for air, hoping for a current to drag me back up, but part of me knew that wouldn't happen. I had seen the last of the sky. I had seen the last of the sun. The remaining rays of light disappeared and I couldn't tell which side was up anymore. The currents tugged me deeper and deeper, spinning me out of control so fast I could hardly move my limbs. Pressure tore them up and down and all around me, wherever the water wanted to make me move. Then a tentacle caught my ankle, wrapping itself up around my leg.

It was keeping me still in the water. Whirls of torrenting blue streaked past me as another tentacle grabbed me by the arm. They began to pull me in opposite directions.

The tentacle dug into my arm, twisting its way inside my skin. It rooted itself into my bone, drilling hard to make leverage for its grip. My shoulder popped out of its socket and I screamed. I could feel and hear my muscles tearing as my arm gave way and my skin ripped like sheets of paper. The tentacle made its way off with my left arm into the dark, leaving a cloud of my blood in the water so dark it looked like hydraulic fluid. I wondered if there was light down here in the dark, if my flesh would look like wires and my bones like the armature used for the animatronics.

Then a light flicked on. Several at the same time.

I looked down and stared at a dozen glowing mechanical eyes tugging what was left of me into their metal mouth.

NO GHOSTS HERE
A. J. Van Belle

Erica had followed Tanner's Uber progress from the airport to her front door, so she flung the door open for him before he could knock. Like a specter dissolved out of the seaside air, he crossed the threshold of her apartment and wrapped her in a hug. He studied her face with melting intensity. He was even more beautiful than she remembered, his long, fair hair too silky, too perfect for a human being. His smooth skin had a luster like no one else's. As if more than his share of aliveness infused him, its light barely contained within the shell of his flesh, struggling to shine forth like a flashlight from behind a curtain.

"You're here." She heard the note of wonder in her voice, as if she hadn't known for sure whether he was still real and could really come to her.

He nodded, expression bright and hopeful. Tearing his gaze away from her, he gave the apartment an obligatory once-over. "Nice place you have. And I love the fact it's on the shore."

"Thanks. It's a new building. The landlady joked it's so new there are no ghosts in this place—she said it was one of the selling points." She kept her voice light, not ready to tell him there *was* a ghost. Not of someone who'd died, but of someone unborn. She sensed the presence every evening, and especially strongly now. It felt like a glowing green light hovering just behind her shoulder, welcoming Tanner into the abode with eager approval.

Tanner pressed his chest and belly to hers, grazed his fingers along her jaw, and kissed her in a way too slow, too lingering, to do anything but promise more—so much more—to come.

When he pulled away, he spent long seconds looking at her, silent. His face radiated joy at their reunion, but something about his gaze felt wrong. There was a coldness in his eyes. Maybe she just wasn't used to seeing him in person in the months since she moved away for a job that turned out not worth the cross-country relocation—not worth being away from Tanner. She'd only dated him for a few weeks before she left, but he'd called her every night since then, and when he asked her to marry him, she didn't even mind that he asked over text. Of course she said yes.

He took her face between his hands. "I've missed you so much." He kissed her again, deep and long, and she didn't know how she could have imagined anything wrong. Being with him again was bliss. "I want to start a family with you right away," he said between kisses. "I can't wait until we're married."

The thought filled her with warmth. She felt the invisible presence's green light glow more brightly with joy at being wanted, welcomed. She was ready, and her baby was ready to come to her, too. But she'd spent her life cautious about pregnancy so, out of habit, she said, "Are you sure?"

He rested his forehead against hers. "Of course

I'm sure. You, and our future baby, are all I want from this world. Can we go to the beach?"

Minutes later, they were on a blanket on the sand, under stars strung like fairy lights through the heavens. She could still feel the nearness of the baby who wanted to be born to her—to them.

As they kissed, his shoulders shook with mounting tension, and she rested a trembling hand on his hair. "You're too perfect to be real," she told him.

"That's because I'm one of the Fair Folk," he said, breathless, undressing her. He stroked her cheek. "You know, the mystical race of not-quite-human beings that would have died out long ago if not for stealing infusions of human blood and spirit."

She laughed and kissed the top of his head. "Silly." And then blinked at the somehow perfectly natural feeling that there were three beings present, even if only two of them had bodies. She pushed Tanner gently onto his back. Rising above him, she drank in the sight of the gorgeous man stretched out below her, all hers.

He should have been all coldness, his washed-out eyes, his ice-pale hair. But his skin burned against hers, his tongue hot. On her knees, straddling his thigh, she shook with wanting, with something stronger than she'd ever felt before.

A rough tremor shook his body, and his eyes looked far away, like shifting clouds in a rainy sky. He took her hips in his hands and guided her over him and, as she settled onto him, she gasped at sensation so intense it felt like a flash of brightness all around her, hiding the corners of the room in blinding white light. She gripped his shoulders and he thrust in a slow rhythm, and under the harmony of their combined breathing she heard something, not with her ears but with her mind and heart.

It sounded like a voice, reaching to her from somewhere beyond the limits of physical matter, beyond space and time as she knew it. Not the sound but the meaning, pulsed into her thoughts.

Mommy. . .I need you.

The baby. The child. The being who was always here with them, whenever they made love. Always here with *her*. The child who pressed so strongly against the veil of darkness between the world of form and the vast nothingness beyond.

She must be imagining the voice. But the presence was so strong, as real an invisible shape in the darkness as his chest under her cheek. So the words spilled out. "I feel her. The child who wants to be born to us."

He shifted, pressing his cheek against the top of her head. He must think she was spouting nonsense, perhaps that she was half asleep already. But the movement of his head—was that a nod? "Me too," he whispered. He kissed her again, and heat flared through her body. It made her vision hazy, made her dizzy and unsure of the line between reality and the world within her mind.

The air shimmered, and through the mist clinging to her eyelashes she saw a hazy place that appeared to be under the sea. Muted sun rays passed through the water and illuminated sparkling people who mingled between pearlescent currents that flowed around them. Otherworldly music hummed at the threshold of hearing, and voices murmured but she couldn't make out the words.

She blinked and sucked in a deep breath, thinking she must be dreaming, must have drifted off here in Tanner's arms. But the strange impression remained, of somewhere else, as real as this beach but beyond the reach of her fingertips.

"What—?" she said aloud, unsure how to ask if this was some imagining or if he sensed it too.

"Shsh." His lips moved over her neck, her collarbone. When he lifted his head, his eyes were paler than ever as he stretched himself along her, chest to chest, and made love to her with strong, determined thrusts. He came with a single low moan. When he withdrew, propped himself on one arm, and looked into her face again, his expression was intense and hopeful.

She circled her thumb over his wrist. "Just think," she said. "That could have been it. I mean, maybe it could take months of trying. But maybe not. We could be having a baby."

He sat back on his heels at the edge of the blanket. Sand clung to his ankles. "I have a feeling we could be." The tender presence of the not-yet-child blew over Erica like a warm wind. "In fact—" Tanner's eyes seemed to glow gold. "It's time."

Another wave of sensation washed over her, this one unfamiliar, as if unseen parts of her were being rearranged, as if her whole existence, body and spirit, were being remade from the foundation. He shifted her onto her back and she let him move her wherever he would. A whirlwind of feeling stormed inside her. Movement in every cell. A tugging sensation in the center of her being, as if a vacuum were pulling the marrow from her bones.

She closed her eyes. Everything spun. Images of DNA helices flashed through her thoughts, dreamlike, the intertwined helix strands ripped apart, duplicating, doubling again and again until she was lost in a sea of thousands of copies of genetic code. Hers and Tanner's, meeting, marrying, forming something new. *This isn't how it's supposed to be.*

The pulling sensation grew and intensified, until everything hurt, to her core, to the matrix of bone in her vertebrae. Her body changed, distorted, swelled. Vaguely, she sensed Tanner was no longer touching her. And still something pulled her even when she had nothing left to give. She reached out with limp fingers, hoping to find Tanner's hand, but there was nothing, only the blanket beneath her atop shifting sand. Above her there was nothing but stars, darkness, and the briny night wind.

Something moved inside her. Was that a baby's kick? Could it be—somehow—the real thing, a pregnancy happening at the speed of light? Muscles cramped, muscles she didn't know she had, and she stopped fumbling for Tanner and concentrated only on surviving the pain ripping her apart.

Through it all, she felt the ghost of the baby closer, closer, becoming part of her now. In her mind's eye she saw a future for herself and the child: a plump, grinning baby perhaps a year old, sitting in a shopping cart, making eye contact with her.

That image faded, and she felt herself sitting on the edge of a bed with a young child cuddled close. She breathed through the pain and fell into the vision of the slender arms around her and the tiny, sweet presence. Of a soft head pressed against her side while she read a bedtime story. The vision lasted only an instant, but she saw and felt every detail: the shell-pink bedspread, the murmur of her own voice in her chest as she read, the child's small fingers spread on her wrist. As if to say, *I don't need to hold tight because I know you won't go anywhere.*

The vision changed, moving forward in time, and she saw herself standing on a green lawn next to a person the same height as herself. A teenager with her own light-brown skin and hair a cool brown somewhere between her own mahogany and Tanner's sun-whitened strands.

She clung to the shifting visions. Through them, she rode waves of pain beyond any torture she could have imagined. The teenager faded, replaced by a young woman, walking along a beach next to Erica, a flop-eared hound loping next to them. The young woman laughed, and clouds of the baby's loving presence were all around Erica, filling the bedroom with joy that said, *I get to be born to you! Mommy, I'm so happy. This is going to be our life! You see it too?*

Yes, Erica thought as wild, burning pain ripped her body in half. *I see it.*

Tanner cupped his hands between her thighs, and his posture seemed wrong to Erica, even through her joy at being united with the baby. The hunch of his spine, the waiting curves of his hands, were a grotesque caricature of earlier gestures meant for pleasure. The pain fled her body, and with it came a tide of blood that soaked into the mattress beneath her and seeped into the blanket crumpled beneath her. But she didn't care about the pain, because sheltered in Tanner's hands was a perfect, tiny baby girl, face scrunched, skin faintly purple blushing to red. And the ghost of the baby, she was here. On this beach. In the flesh, a ghost no more. The warm, loving pulse of the child's presence permeated the small body and reached out toward Erica. She felt as if a warm, green light encompassed her heart. She struggled to sit up, weak and torn but not caring because here was the child she'd come to know over the past months. The baby that was already hers in spirit, now here in body. She didn't know how the baby had come to be all in one night, but she didn't care because she was here—oh, she was *here*.

A small, wrinkled pink fist uncurled and reached for Erica. Tanner got to his feet in a smooth motion, holding the baby out of Erica's reach, its tiny, fragile head soft against his own chest. He took another step from her, toward the water's foamy edge. She managed to stand and stepped off the blanket to follow him, but weakness made her slow, and he remained out of reach.

He pulled out something gossamer and shimmery, though she couldn't see where it came from. The thin object's folds floated on the air. Weightless, it glittered as if made of starlight. A papery square of something not substantial enough to be called fabric, it was the right size to serve as a baby blanket. Tanner wrapped the infant with care and tenderness. The baby—Erica's baby—cooed and turned its face toward her, blinking with clear, impossibly lavender eyes.

"This blanket will protect her in the crossing

of the veil." There was something terrible and grim underneath Tanner's voice, though his tone remained calm and level.

He looked different. Hair no longer sun-bleached blond to mere pallor but jagged, sharp, like shards of ice, white against the warmth of his skin. And his chest and shoulders, crisscrossed with scars. She had a brief flash of him out on the open ocean, swimming like a shark, chasing dolphins made of sea foam across the waves. Grappling with one. Flesh ripped by claws of ocean mist.

He cradled the wriggling baby to his chest. With the blanket around her tiny body, Erica's newborn daughter looked like a bundle of starlight. All the years, the hopes, everything she'd seen over the course of her life, was wrapped in that bundle. It was everything.

A tall wave rushed toward shore and stood still without crashing to the sand. It formed a wall of water in front of Tanner. He stepped through that shimmering wall as if it were a rift in the fabric of everything. Erica saw through the spacetime crevice into that other dimension she'd glimpsed before. In it, people hovered in wavering currents, sparking green and purple. She blinked hard but they were still there, with fins in place of toes and fingers. Erica stepped forward, but the air formed an invisible wall and stopped her.

The people in the shining underwater dimension turned and greeted Tanner with open hands and gentle faces. They were all tall, ethereal, with long hair too silky to be real, just like his. Long fins trailed from their fingers and toes and they hovered, treading water. Erica tried again to follow him but still couldn't move. She watched in paralyzed agony as the beautiful, terrible underwater beings exclaimed over her baby for long minutes, until Tanner handed the child to waiting hands that took the bundle with infinite gentleness.

He stepped back through the rip in the spacetime and it closed seamlessly behind him. The wave fell back and rejoined the ocean, erasing all trace of that ocean world. The place where the ocean met the sand was no longer a veil to the beyond. All Erica saw in front of her was sea and the night air.

Tanner looked ordinary again—or as ordinary as he ever had. He still glowed with that strange almost-light, but now she could have seen him on the street and not noticed anything but a man. Particularly handsome, perhaps, but not from another world. He ran a hand through his hair and the strands clung to each other like cobwebs before falling past his ears.

Erica felt as insubstantial as the faint shimmer that divided her world from his. "What are you?" she whispered. "And what just happened?"

He looked down at the ground as he spoke in a low monotone. "I told you what I am, you know. You didn't believe me. I even told you all I wanted from *this* world were you—for now—and the child we would have. The children born to the Folk in our realm are sickly. The flesh is solid, but the spirit-stuff of our kind is stretched thin. Our babies lack life force, so they weaken and die. The child you and I have created together will thrive, because she's part of your spirit. And you, primitive human that you are, have a strong life force indeed."

A gale-force wind of loss blew through Erica's empty chest. "But she knows I'm her mother. She was calling for me. You felt it, too!"

He raised his head to look her in the eye, and she saw no hint of warmth or humanity in his gaze. "She'll forget," he said in the same monotone. "In the way all children have of forgetting. They're wise beyond measure at conception and infancy. Physically powerless, but with infinite vision. They lose that as soon as they gain speech, thankfully. Otherwise toddlers would be even more beastly to control."

"If she's wise beyond measure—and she said she needs me, then she—"

"Best not to think about it. Your human mind is too small to comprehend the needs of the Folk. Trying will only hurt you. Now that you know, you should forget too. Most of my breeding women do. They end up thinking it was all a dream. Or so I've been told." He scooped his pile of discarded clothing and shook the sand out of his pants. "I'll be going."

"You're not—staying? You came all this way." Her tongue felt thick, her words clumsy and stupid. "Aren't we. . .engaged?"

He bit his lower lip, and he seemed to be using the gesture as a ploy, trying and failing to appear innocent. Something that was not quite sadness crossed his face. "You shouldn't have trusted me." He pulled on his clothes. Buttoned his shirt with long, slender fingers. "But, to be fair to you, I'm very good at my work. My people wouldn't survive if it weren't for what I do."

He headed up the beach toward the row of dark buildings. She followed him for a few paces, leaving the blanket behind her. "The—" Her mouth was too dry for speech. She swallowed and tried again. "The. . .baby?" Or the ghost of a baby. It had substance; it tore her in half. There was nothing physical here to show for it. Yet it was real. It had to be. He'd felt it too. He'd held it in his hands.

"I'm sorry." He turned back toward her and kissed her forehead. "The only time that's real is now. And, now, there are no ghosts here. Unborn or otherwise."

"I saw. I know what you are. You told me yourself: you didn't even lie to me about it. I could tell people what you've done."

He backed away from her, a faint, cruel smile on his face. "Who's going to believe you?"

"But what will I tell—my—my coworkers? They were so excited because I was—" She couldn't manage the word *engaged* again.

His joyless smile showed his canines. "Tell them I'm an immature asshole who lured you in but got scared of commitment. It's the truth anyway, if you look at it in a certain light."

He walked away and, as she watched him go, she put a hand over her breastbone. Her fingers grew cold, haunted by the hollow where something might have been. He breezed up the beach to the point where it met the gravel road, where he disappeared from sight. She stood still, unable to feel her feet touching the sand. Unable to feel anything at all besides a gaping emptiness inside.

She swayed against night air filled with the smell of the sea and the haze of starlight. Maybe none of it was real. A dream.

She turned away from it, from him, toward the infinity of the ocean. It couldn't have been real. *Tell them I'm an immature asshole.* That was the truth. The *only* truth. It had to be.

She ran her hands down her body again, cupping the taut, slight curve of her belly. This was not the body of someone who'd just carried a baby to term. She slipped a finger between her legs. There was no pain, no numbness, no swelling from the punishment of giving birth. And, on her finger when she held it up to the light, no blood.

It wasn't real, then. It was a fever dream, something that popped like a mushroom from the fetid darkness of a mind bent by confusion.

It must be late. She had work in the morning. Although too numb to care, she should try to get some sleep.

She trudged over to retrieve the blanket. By starlight, the blanket looked strangely dark. She knelt next to it for a better look. The darkness was uneven, like—bloodstains. She lifted its thick fabric and found it heavy with wetness. Red handprints dotted the edges, and the center of the blanket was soaked through, sodden with her gore.

The air above the blanket rippled. Shimmered green for a moment. Through the green, she saw a child's face, untouchable as if through a pane of thick glass, but features perfectly sharp. The little girl wore an expression of infinite sadness and resignation. Her eyes had the vacancy of a thousand-yard stare.

Erica reached out a hand, and the child's gaze focused on her.

You were supposed to be my mommy. . .

Even as the words slipped into her mind, the green mist evaporated, and the rip in spacetime vanished. Erica stood alone with a future that would never be, a beach empty but for the evidence of blood she never shed, and the nightmare memory of a child that never was.

AND IN HER EYES, THE END
Melissa Pleckham

When you find me, I will be bloated with salt and sea. I will look like I've been underwater for a week, a month. When you find me, you will wonder how this could happen, just a few days out from that last time I was sighted on land.

When you find me, my mouth will be full of seaweed. It will hang from between my lips, greenish-brown and bloated. When you find me, you will try to shake me awake, and the fat bladders will burst in my mouth and fetid water will dribble down my chin. You will turn away and heave.

When you find me, I will be the last man standing. Not alive, you see. But standing.

When you find me, you will find her, crouched in some corner. Her eyes look afraid but her teeth are sharp. She is beautiful. You will kneel down beside her.

She will drown you. She will try. But — keep swimming.

Keep swimming.

* * *

As a boy, I loved the sea. I grew up on the beach; the land was an afterthought, a promise made by the low tide and destroyed by the high tide. The land was unreliable. The sea was unpredictable, but honest. It never pretended to be more than it was. It never pretended to be safe.

My father was like me: tall, dark-haired, drawn to the water. My mother could not hold us down, could not dry us out. My father would take me into the sea, on the days when a storm turned the sky gray-green and the waves roiled like men fighting in the tavern after too many ales. We never swam together on days when the see was calm and smooth like glass — only when a storm was coming. My mother would stand on the beach and call to us; she would open her arms wide and wrap a towel around my shoulders when I emerged, shivering, my lips chattering, the hairs on my arms erect, my hair salt-stringed and swollen. She would cast my father dirty looks and wrap me in the towel and take me inside and feed me clam chowder from a cauldron suspended over the fire. He would glare back and say, "What did you learn today, boy? What did I teach you?" and I would say, "Keep swimming, Father," and he would say, yes, whatever else you do, yes, keep swimming. Keep swimming. Keep your head above water, keep swimming.

He was a fisherman, my father. He made his life in the sea, but when you say *fisherman* to one who doesn't know, they think of a hunter, but really he was more like a shaman. A priest. He didn't hunt or pillage, he asked, and bartered, and supplicated, and pleaded. He taught me all I ever knew.

"There are things in the sea, boy," he'd said, "that you could never understand. Things that will end you. All you can do is keep your head above water. Keep breathing dry air."

I was there on the day he drowned.

We took the trawler out together at sunrise, but at sunset I sailed back alone. The storm swept in earlier than expected, and a rogue wave had ripped him overboard, tossed him from the deck. I watched him go under, then come up, gasping for air, reaching for me. I clung to what I could, tried not to go over myself. The sea thundered and roared, but over the din I still heard his last words: "Keep swimming," he'd screamed, and I couldn't be sure I'd really heard it, maybe it was all in my mind. "Keep swimming, keep swimming." His lips moved but there was no more sound save the waves. His mouth opened and closed like a fish stranded on a deck. I watched him go under again, for the last time. He did not come back up.

When I told my mother, she swayed, but she did not go down. She aspirated but she did not drown.

* * *

Manhood meant the ship was now mine. She had a small crew — fewer than half a dozen on any given day. We sailed the same seas I had known since childhood, the seas that had taken my father, the seas that had given me everything I'd had and taken everything I'd known.

Did I like the sea? There's a question I'd never been asked. Does a prisoner like his cage? No, I resented it, but I accepted it. It was all I'd ever known. My mother had died years before; without my father, she hadn't much to live for. A son is no substitute. I had never taken a wife.

On cold, lonely days I would gaze out at the horizon and think: *keep swimming. Keep swimming.* It kept my mind clear. I knew what I had to do.

One morning, like any other morning, from the deck of the trawler we spotted a ship. She was still and silent in the fog like a lighthouse looming, but in the middle of the sea, miles from shore. We pulled alongside her and boarded her, to see if anyone needed help.

On a chair below deck, we found him. His face was swollen and distended, his flesh mottled and moldered. He looked as though he'd drowned, but there was no water anywhere in the cabin, save for the water dripping from his eyes, down his chin. "What's this?" my first mate breathed, and reached out quivering fingers to pull a length of kelp from the man's ear. My mate screamed and dropped his torch. I gazed, amazed.

From behind us, we heard a sound. I want to say I heard it first, but we turned at the same time. There was a woman crouched behind a desk, her long red hair soaked blood-black. Her eyes were sea-green and downcast. She was nude, and shaking. Her hair was so long it covered her breasts, her back. I knelt down beside her.

"Hello," I said. "Hello. Are you alright?"

She looked up at me, shaking, and smiled. Her teeth looked sharp.

I shivered.

* * *

There was a vote before we let her on board. Women are bad luck on a ship ("Who decided that?" my mother had asked sharply. "Probably someone who'd met a woman," my father hissed).

Despite the superstition, we voted four to one to allow her on board. I was the only dissent.

The vessel was mine, so our boarder became mine too. I cared for her — I did. I pitied her. I clothed her, I fed her. She didn't speak; I carried her. Too weak to walk, I ferried her from deck to cabin and back again. She held close to me, leaning her head against my chest. She smelled like the sea, brackish and bracing, not sweet. She smelled like a thousand mysteries, a million unknowable depths. She looked at me and smiled, her teeth small and pointed. When waves broke on the bough she cried. Once, I saw her wave to dolphins as they threaded through the water like slippery needles through cloth.

I wanted her. I wanted her.

At night, she watched the moon trail through the black waves behind the ship. At night, her green eyes looked as black and bottomless as those waves.

The sight of the ocean at night always filled me with an indescribable, knee-weakening dread. It was like catching a glimpse into an abyss that would consume me whole if it wanted to. I tried not to gaze at it for very long. I tried to avert my eyes unless absolutely necessary.

Sometimes I looked at her like that. That same primordial awe, that dread I felt for the blackest ocean. I could feel that for her if I let myself.

She ate the fish we gave her whole. She ate

them raw.

She never spoke, or told us her name. She never told us anything at all.

I wanted her.

* * *

One morning, before the sun, I awoke to a song. The singing was so sweet, and so sad. There was no music, only a voice. I pulled on my trousers and followed that voice to the deck, where the waves lashed the wood. I hadn't seen my crew — how long had it been? An hour, a day, a week? I shook my head.

I saw her, perched on the bow. Her breasts were bare, her skin luminescent in the darkness, as if they were lit from within. She looked like a figurehead carved from Italian marble — smooth and hard. She glowed like a lighthouse, like the full moon. I moved toward her, transfixed.

When I reached her, she stepped down and smiled. She turned toward me and bared her teeth, her jaw clenched. Her teeth were rubied red with gore and viscera. I wanted to scream but I didn't know how. She held out her hand toward me and I met it with my own. Our fingers laced together. Her skin was scaled and firm like a salmon. Her sin was iridescent. I wanted to scream but I'd forgotten how.

She pulled me close. *Keep swimming, keep swimming.*

Her lips pressed into mine; it was all I'd wanted since we'd found that ship, all I'd longed for. It felt like fog parting to show me the land when I'd been lost at sea; it felt like bursting out of the surface of the water when the waves had kept me under too long. She parted my lips with her tongue and I wanted to gasp, I wanted to breathe her in. I wanted to drown.

Keep swimming.

Keep swimming.

I heard him then, all at once, in my head. My father. Quietly at first. Then louder. Then louder. My eyes fluttered open, my hands released hers. I staggered backwards, but she wove her fingers into my hair and sealed her mouth onto mine. A wave crashed over us; from the corner of my vision, a flapping, as of a fin. Her legs gave way, or she otherwise ceased to stand somehow. We tumbled to the deck together. She pinned me, her mouth still on mine. I wriggled like a fish. My eyes, stunned, opened wide.

I must confess, she is all I'd ever wanted. I'd never wanted anyone else.

I must confess, you see. Because when I died, I was not forgiven. Because she took me then. And as she kissed me, my mouth filled with saltwater. My mouth filled with saltwater and with the sea, and the sea spilled from my nose and my mouth. The sea ran down my chin, out my eyes. *Keep swimming*, I thought. But faintly now. *Keep swimming.*

A pressure built in my head, a dull throb deep within my sinuses, then a soft pop and I could feel the seaweed snake out of my nose, my ears, I could feel it climb up my throat and tie my tongue to hers. She kissed me more deeply and I gagged, I reeled. *Keep swimming*, I thought. *Keep swimming, keep swimming.*

That morning I learned: there is more than one way to drown.

* * *

When you find me, you will wonder at the improbability of my situation. How could a man drown on the dry deck of a ship, his entire crew unaccounted for? How could his body be bloated and brined? How could this happen?

When you find me, you will find her. She will be kneeling nearby. You will know her by her sad eyes, by her silent laugh, by her hair that blazes like a fire on the horizon. You will know her because she is the sea personified and you will fear her. You will want her too.

When you find me, you will not know how a man can meet his end as I met mine. But when you look into her eyes, you will understand.

Keep swimming. Keep swimming.

As for me, I am swimming still. But in the dark, the deep dark.

As for you?

Keep swimming.

THE AEQUOR
H.M. Lightcap

Log date: 3/15/15
Location: Cape Town (South Sandwich Trench)
Vessel: Aequor (Prototype Beta 2.18.1)

The click of an old camcorder is heard before the scene loads slowly, revealing an older woman sitting in the cerulean glimmer of the ocean light. The quality is somewhat grainy but legible. The oscillating refractions make her wide eyes darker and more exotic. Her hair is dark and curly, with white strands laced through that dip and weave like the sea she's surrounded by. Wrinkles caress her eyes and mouth as she grins exuberantly. Playful curiosity and excitement play on her face despite her age.

"Hello, I'm Doctor Edwina Lark. I'm a marine biologist working with engineers at Pantheon on a prototype submarine. It's pretty rudimentary in terms of tech!" Edwina teases, leaning conspiratorially towards the camera. "This is the first official launch into the deep ocean to see if the simulations and tests hold up. As such, I don't have anything deemed unnecessary. I've got the submarine, my lunch, a blanket, some books and stuff I tossed in a bag, and some lights." Edwina flicks her cabin lights on and off jokingly.

"Dr. Lark, you're all hooked up. Prepare for the descent."

Edwina sticks her tongue out at the speaker.

"There's also a one-way communicator," she explains. "I don't have a radio. To be fair, there wasn't supposed to be a real person on this voyage. I might have bullied my way on at the last minute. But I wouldn't have done it if I didn't have total faith in the engineers up top!" Edwina grabs the camera and maneuvers it on the tripod to peek around the top of the submarine. The camera takes time to focus but, eventually, a chain laced with cable comes into focus. It turns quickly back to her.

"That tracks all the monitors for the pressure points they're testing for structural integrity. If anything goes wrong, they'll haul me up in no time! If they don't, I signed a waiver anyway!" Edwina adds jokingly. There's a jolt as the chain slowly lowers the submarine. The clangs echo through the water, but the distortion makes it sound less mechanical and more rhythmic, like growling. She once again rotates the camera, focusing on the bottom of a massive ship. The grain of the camera makes it appear rusty as the submarine sinks too fast for the lens to focus on the barnacles and sea life.

"We're in the epipelagic zone, for everyone watching this after the voyage. It's shallow, only two hundred meters." Edwina demonstrates this by tilting the camera downward in the bubbled window. A rapidly approaching navy blue glow softens the blow of impending darkness. She rights it back to its original position. "We're going to be together for a while. I know you're on loan to track the mission, but

I think I'll give you a name." She flirts with the camera, waving her finger at the lens like it's a small animal. She frowns in mock thought and holds her chin.

"Brian? No, you look too old to be a Brian. Chadwick? No. I have an ex named Chad. I don't feel like getting into that when I'm alone in a small, dark, enclosed space, trapped for an unknown amount of time. What about Cassian? That's a fun name! Classy, too, good for an old boy like you. I tease you about your age, but I should be grateful you aren't some new-fangled fancy nonsense." She grabs Cassian and puts it up to her face. "Let me give you a tour while we still have light. That's the window; it's almost three hundred and sixty degrees. Except for these parts here." She points at the roof and main ballast tanks, leaving an awkward window shaped like a natal star. The front of the capsule faces a ridge of the plateau of South Sandwich Trench, giving Edwina Lark a view to look at. It's less imposing than the open ocean, and they want her in the capsule as long as possible.

"Here's my bench! It seats three, and it's made of leather. Very fancy, as you can see!" Edwina emphasized by laying out on it, posing gaily. She sits up again and points at the control panel. "This is where the magic happens. Don't worry, I won't touch it. It has power in case of an emergency. That doesn't help me because I don't know anything about steering, but the thought is nice." Edwina puts Cassian back in the camera stand at the top of the control panel.

"And finally, there's little old me," Edwina

discloses with a wave of her hand. Light fades quickly as it's slowly choked out by water.

"*Achieved 1000 meters*," the monotone male voice announces.

"Hey! That means we're in the mesopelagic zone or the twilight zone." She flutters her fingers creepily. The clangs of the chain sound deeper now, like rocks falling from the ridge. "Well, I'm here for the long haul. I'll slip into something comfortable. What do you say, gentlemen?" she says, and takes out a sweatshirt from her bag. She slips it on and kicks off her shoes, lounging on the leather bench, enjoying the last of the sunlight. Watching the alabaster glow disappear makes the drop go by faster than before. Anxiety twists Edwina's face briefly before it all goes black.

* * *

Curses and scuffles ring out before the light turns on. It's small and dim compared to the surrounding darkness.

"*Achieved 2000 meters*."

"The Bathypelagic zone. The midnight zone," she clarifies. "I've never been this deep before. It's exciting but nerve-wracking." The sounds of the chain are nonexistent. All that's left is a heavy meditative silence. Edwina's face is too far from the light to see, but her bare feet curl and flex, squeaking on the sticky material. "I probably shouldn't have blown through all my conversation topics within the first five minutes, huh?" she muses. Edwina takes out a tablet from her bag. She turns it on and is immediately blinded. From the reflection in the window, we can see she turned on the battery saver and started playing solitaire.

* * *

"Achieved 5000 meters."

Edwina jerks and fumbles with her tech in surprise. "Already?" I guess time flies when you do absolutely nothing." Edwina looks at the camera. "That puts us in the abyss. Usually, it takes forty-five minutes to an hour to get this deep. They're probably in a hurry to drop us to the entire testing area with high oceanic pressure." She settles back in and fidgets.

"Maybe I should try to sleep," Edwina states out loud, shutting down her tablet and turning off the light. A whine leaves Cassian, as Edwina leans close to the camera, fiddling with buttons to switch it to night vision, muttering prayers.

Circular glowing eyes reflect through a roof window of the submarine. A noseless, white, humanoid face with barbels branching from the cheeks stares impassively. Webbed and tentacled hand-like appendages press against the glass. The creature opens its lipless maw, allowing its protrusible jaw to extend, releasing rows of jagged fangs. They flex and stretch them menacingly.

Edwina's face twitches in thought before sighing and turning off night vision. She turns the lights back on. The creature has disappeared into the abyss.

"Storm in. . .contr-emergen. . ." The static

announcement trails off.

Edwina's face goes pale, and she grips her seat. The steady drop halts, rattling the submarine. For the first time, she's feeling the pressure.

Then she drops.

Edwina has an urgent death grip on her seat. Her back is arching, and her bottom rears up as she struggles to remain grounded.

Clangs of the chain ring like dinner bells as it struggles to save the machinery. Despite the soft leather, she lands hard with a bone-shaking impact. Edwina grabs the edge of the control panel as the drop stops, and the swaying begins. The chain swings slowly as it rights itself from the fall.

"I want off this ride right now!" She groans in frailty. Indiscriminate insults are flung at the engineers, the submarine, the sea, and all its creatures until the swaying subsides. Desperate for a grounding force, she buries her face in her arm.

Looking green, Edwina lifts her head from her forearm. She grabs her blanket from the bag and curls in on herself, childlike, closing her eyes. Her muscles twitch from the pain and adrenaline. Deep breaths are the only sound heard after the links settle.

"You're OK. Nothing is broken; everything is fine. The guys are topside, and they will get us soon," she tells herself, turning towards the camera.

"How are you feeling, Cass? Filming everything OK?" Her eyes draw to something behind the camera. With pain and motion sickness momentarily forgotten, she leans forward with narrowing eyes. "What is that?"

Cassian is turned outward to the window. A

duo of formless bioluminescent masses are pulsing feebly.

"Should I?" Fumbling and tapping ensue in the background. "I am a scientist, after all. What kind of a woman of biology would I be if I didn't?"

The spotlight flicks on. Edwina stifles a gasp of shock. A disgustingly human-like figure kneels in an alcove. The head is large compared to its slim shoulders. Its serene expression, eyes, and shut mouth leave it almost featureless. Transparent, flexible spines frame it like an elegant mane of hair. Its torso is bony but smooth and white, with large gills lining the floater ribs. On the belly of the creature, two fetal tumor-like growths latch on either side.

Their heads are fully grown, but their bodies are tiny and atrophied, easily one-fifth the size of the host. The skin is translucent and sits in sharp contrast to the solid figure. Delicate needle-thin bones make up the visible spine and arms. Their mouths are obscured by their bulbous heads, but a mist of black miasma hangs in the water around the creature.

Gaunt arms carefully clutch the mucus sack on their lap. Everything occupies such a small space it's impossible to tell what's birthing and fertilizing. Their hands are boneless tentacles that massage and seem to comfort the newborns. The bottom of their body isn't visible through the matte mesh filling with oblong white embryos. Undeveloped black eyes occasionally rise to the surface.

The creature lifts its head and opens its eyes. Baseball-sized black globes suck in the light and stare into the submarine. They curl in on their sack protectively and straighten their spines in a warning.

Their mouth cracks open, revealing tiny teeth. The carnassial teeth begin chattering, accompanied by panting that flexes their gills and expands their ribs. The camera shakes and turns back to Edwina.

Humanoid figures appear from the darkness, illuminated by the residual spotlight glow. Some are immediately threatening with flexed razor teeth and writhing fingers. Some seem relaxed and curious. Others are wary and somewhere in between. It is impossible to see how many there are due to the flurry of white and gray scales with clear spines carrying the darkness of the abyss. A cacophony of monochromia broken up by the sky blue glow of tumorous growths jealously guarded by their host.

Edwina stares open-mouthed at the display. The scientist in her is elated and fascinated. The person is terrified. "What do I do? Can they see me?" she whispers to Cassian. "Oh God, what if they can hear me?" Silent tears stream down her face. She wipes her nose.

The submarine shakes, and she cries harder, whimpering. The chain groans, agitating the school further.

The birthing pod closes itself farther and chatters louder. Clattering and gnashing of teeth respond in kind at a maddening pace. Innumerable echoes from the natural shape of the alcove resound and join the communications—the cadence of the huffs conglomerates into a primitive song.

Edwina could appreciate the beauty if she knew whether the shaking was the humanoids or the stalled crane of the ship.

Another shake rocks her back and forth more

violently. All fall silent. She turns the camera out, facing the hull.

The largest birthing partner grabs rocks and dirt and flings them at the submarine.

The swarm descends. Tentacles sucker themselves to the glass, and teeth fully extend into prongs and tines of bone, attempting purchase on the smooth surface—a lucky few attempt to gnaw on the metal of the roof and ballast tanks.

The camera turns back to her. Edwina is shaking and staring into space. A loud clunk assaults her ear. Edwina scrambles back, piling herself as far from the glass as she can.

"They have rocks. They're going to break in!" The thunk of glass gets more frequent and louder. The submarine shakes and rocks. She balances precariously and puts her hand out to grab Cassian from the tripod. Edwina tries multiple times before eventually grabbing it in time to see the cracking glass. They've broken through the first layer. They rip away the hull to begin on the second.

Aequor begins to rise. The frenzy becomes more desperate. Furious teeth and rocks crack the glass, and the submarine begins taking on water.

"Bring me up faster! Hurry up! Aren't your stupid sensors going off?" she demands as water floods the cabin. The creatures break the spotlight, plunging Edwina into disorienting darkness beyond her cabin light. Metallic scrapes signal further vandalism.

Cassian shakes and struggles to remain focused as Edwina rummages in her bag, looking for anything to help. The lens catches brief glimpses of suckers adhering and disappearing with boney white teeth smacking for purchase against the glass. Black rocks chip away at the final layer of protective acrylic.

Edwina is wielding a metal water bottle like a club. The thick design fits awkwardly in her hand, but it's good enough. She wipes her tears and snot away with a sleeve, and a look of steely determination takes hold.

A loud shatter shakes her resolve. The camera turns away from Edwina and faces the impending complication. There's a hole in the acrylic straining to stay closed, but the scaled head of a beast is pushing in teeth first. The protruding jaw momentarily protects it from the glass shards, but eventually it's forced to retreat. Water flows freely, infecting the cabin with liquid darkness.

Edwina sits hunched on top of her seat, wrapped in her blanket. Cold water sucks out what little warmth she has left. Arms try to reach in but are thwarted by the shards, giving an unexpected layer of protection. Their blood is red, dripping on the glass and control panel, and occasionally splatters on the seat she's perched atop. It all turns black as it makes contact with the water.

Heaves of breath and clattering of jaws change in speed and pitch. Clearly a form of communication, but it leaves no hints for Edwina to interpret her fate or their plans. The only saving grace in their violence is that as they reach for her, they inadvertently plug the hole of her demise with their limbs and faces.

The one-way communication gurgles weakly as the speaker clogs with blood and flailing tentacles, grabbing it for purchase. However, the burgles signal hope for Edwina, and she stares out the roof, hoping for some kind of light or sign that the turmoil is over. The hope is short-lived.

A change in tactic trickles through her assailants. Stones chip away at the hole and widen it enough for a creature to get its head and shoulders in. It gasps and wheezes in victory to its comrades. Its torso and arms bleed profusely as it writhes to wrestle more of its body inside. The cabin light is blotted out in the flood, ominously silhouetting the intruder.

Ligaments in their jaw flex and protrude their fangs inches away from Edwina's face, fanning the stench of rot and decay across their face. As it gets within arm's reach, Edwina brings her water bottle down on its head in a panic. The wound bleeds, but it's not enough damage to stop them.

The flood has swelled to her waist, giving further advantage to the predators. The intruder is flailing, driven mad by pain and animal instincts. Their head and torso slam into the walls and control panel of the tiny space. Their arms are still trapped by the window and withered appendages.

Edwina is holding her water bottle aloft, waiting for the right time to strike again. The radio wordlessly babbles, and a delicate navy glow flows into the atmosphere. The creatures jabber in a new distressed gurgling as the majority begin to retreat.

Withdrawal allows torrents of water to flood the space. It surges up to her chest, and her assailant has enough space to bring their arms into the pod. Edwina screams in an animalistic rage.

Cassian is dropped into the water, and all goes black.

THE TRUTH IS AS INTIMATE AS THE TEETH THAT BIT YOUR LEGS OFF FIRST
Elizabeth R. McClellan

After Sean Barry Parsons

"This is based on my therapy session yesterday
where for some reason I thought
it was a good idea to tell a licensed therapist
all my insane fears about the ocean."

"Stuff in there." Whales older than electricity. Sharks.
The U.S.S. Indianapolis, the screaming days
the final boys who lived discuss on YouTube,
if you're into that. No judgment. Really.

If you've listened to Jade Daniels like you should,
you know Jaws is a slasher, that shark grown
fat off the Little Boy carried by the doomed Indianapolis,
back to set things right by tooth and fin,

back for the fear of sharks carved into
<u>mostly white mostly </u>America, the demonization
blockbuster that almost destroyed an ecology
of dinosaur age, back for a fragile masculine

that jams their teeth in chokers to pick up
girls who love Jimmy Buffett, lays waste
upon the sharks as we have always done,
though they're less dangerous,statistically, than

a loose plug you can't afford to pay the electrician
to come fix, sparking putative house fire.
Fear of fire doesn't embed itself like a megalodon
come to eat the Orca and all who sail in her, vengeful

woman king of apex predation dragged to
unwanted consciousness by hubris, Adam
Frankenstein come back for his slasher revenge
gender swapped, a woman finally biting back,

the vagina dentata of it all, queen come
for the reckoning, ancient cousin of kaiju,
mother of a million sequels, a billion screaming
mouths agape, the ocean's jaws closing.

The problem is there are. . .other things,
than just sharks, who mostly are not vicious,
just struggling to continue against the new ecologies
we gave them, poison in the weave, like we always do.

There are things that live where the sun has no dominion,
who suck heat and light and food in a darkness so total the
tiny flashes in it are the stars
behind your eyes after they hit you,

Hell yes I'm afraid of the ocean and Freud
can go hang. I greet her like a mother with
a mother's power, avoid her like Mom,
stay inland, to the water that wants me.

No good comes of people like us and oceans.
They are not made for me. Reducing
plastic waste, thinking of Tetley and Fuckwits,
dreaming Great Garbage Patch dreams

the size of Texas after the armadillo have
all run to Tennessee to spare the heat.
It's a good life, if you don't weaken.
Don't go around picking fights with someone else's god.

FISHING LICENSE
Grace Daly

The local government is cracking down hard on people fishing without a license. Even with a license, there are limits now to how many fish each boat is permitted to pull out of the inky depths. Conor and Betha's niece says this is a good thing, says it's important for the government to prevent overfishing, says humans need to respect the oceans and let them heal. In Betha's estimation, her niece had gotten awful full of herself during her first two years at Trinity College. Thinks she knows everything. How quickly, how conveniently young, educated people forget that it is the hard labour of working men and women that make their soft lifestyles possible.

Betha spits over the side of the tiny, single-person skiff she'd borrowed, and watches her phlegm disappear into the dark waves. It's dangerous to be out here, alone, at night, but it can't be helped. She can't be caught; she doesn't have a fishing license. Originally, they could only afford the one, and it made more sense to put it in Conor's name. He was the better fisherman.

Of course, she could afford to get herself a fishing license, now Conor's life insurance payout had hit her bank account. She could buy herself all kinds of things. She gazes down at her wedding ring, a thick golden band with an intricate claddagh stamped into the metal. Conor wore a matching one, just the same as hers but bigger; they'd had them custom made. She feels her throat clench tight. All she wants these days, money can't buy. All she wants is Conor's wedding band and Conor himself, safe in her bed, never to sail this briny betrayer of a sea again.

Betha can't have Conor back. The only thing left for her is vengeance. She thinks of the spear gun tucked between her legs, feels the heft of its sturdy wooden stock. Yes, vengeance will satisfy Betha. Waiting for the local government to approve a new fishing license won't. She needed to set out hunting as soon as she realized what had happened to her husband.

Officially, Conor's boat and every man aboard disappeared when they sailed past the limits of the fishing grounds Betha had carefully mapped out for them. Foolish, everyone knows that. A small skiff like the one Conor was captain of couldn't handle the open ocean, where waves crash like felled giants and fierce creatures silently lurk with conveyor belts of teeth. It was Conor's fault for sailing out so far, and at first Betha cursed him for it. How could her husband be so stupid? But this afternoon, it had dawned on her: he wasn't stupid. He was lured.

The rumors have been going on for decades, centuries even. Out in the ocean there are twisted beasts: squids the size of school buses, shrimp that move faster than the speed of sound, fish with lights that dangle from their foreheads to illuminate teeth too sharp and numerous to fit in their own mouths. And, of course, beautiful women with scaled tails capable of singing a man to his doom and devouring his flesh, if they happen to be hungry enough. If the oceans are as overfished as Betha's niece and the government say, the sirens would certainly be hungry.

So Betha made the only logical choice. After buying the spear gun at a local shop and borrowing the solo skiff from her neighbour, she set out into the open midnight sea wearing Conor's spare cap and old Aran sweater. Of course, she's also wearing a fake beard, an uncomfortable cheap one the church had left over from last year's nativity play. She itches at her chin but leaves it be, trusting that the disguise is necessary to lure the loathsome aberration to the surface.

Betha isn't afraid of the siren. Her knowledge of the ocean and its patterns, of where to find the best fishing spots based on the weather and currents, of how to skim over crushing waters, is unparalleled. It's why she and Conor made such a good team. Her studies of the sea had always bordered on obsessive, and the obsession had only grown since her person had been taken from her.

She travels a great distance, farther than a solo skiff should safely go. Conor would be proud to see her now: fierce concentration, corded muscle, and understanding of the sea conquering the battering waves. He had never been one for beautiful women, the sort with willowy waists and pretty words who sit around waiting to be admired. But oh, how he loved Betha, for her vast height and her formidable size, for the things she could do others wouldn't dare. For her lack of social niceties that, even now, affords her the courage to slay the beauty that killed him.

The waves grow calm and she allows herself a moment's rest, turning off the skiff's motor and checking over her supplies under the light of her small lamp. The spear gun looks solid and dependable, the small harpoon securely locked in and the rope firmly attached on both ends. Her knife is sharp, and strapped to her belt on the left side. Scant rations and fresh water, plus a first aid kit and a few flares, are tucked away behind the seat, wrapped in a tarp. Of course, if she ended up in a situation where she needed to eat those rations, she was likely already as good as dead. The open ocean is the worst place to find yourself in need of rescue, and where she is now, placid unknowable water stretches out in all directions to the horizon. But Betha's never needed rescuing before. She does a few quick calculations in her head and guesstimates that she should be approaching near where the siren attacked Conor, if she isn't already past it.

She looks across the expanse to her right and sees something strange on the water's undulating surface, thirty or so meters away. It looks like seaweed attached to the sea floor, reaching up to the surface to gather the sun's rays, but it's too lightly colored to be kelp. Besides, the sea floor is far beneath Betha's flimsy solo skiff. She had just crossed over a drop off (she has all the local drop offs memorized, of course), so the water here must reach about sixty meters down. Maybe more. Betha can't imagine any seaweed rooting at those dark depths, or reaching such a spooling length.

Unbidden, an image of a skull the size of Conor's sinking downdowndown and landing in the dark silt enters Betha's mind. She flinches and the image changes; now the skull rests on the floor, kelp growing through its eye socket, a small crab hunkering inside the jaw. She squeezes her eyes shut and visualizes the pathway of the North Atlantic Drift to calm herself.

When her heart rate is normal and her piercing lonesome heartbreak has quieted to a manageable level, Betha opens her eyes again. She scans the surface of the water on her right for the odd seaweed, but sees nothing. Slower now, she scans ahead of her, then to her left.

There, at seven o'clock, in the left rear quadrant, float the lightly-colored tendrils. Her brow furrows. There's no way the skiff could've spun so quickly without her noticing. The tendrils must have moved. She feels for the grip of the spear gun but she doesn't lift it, not wanting to risk making a sound and scaring off whatever it might be.

Betha wishes she could see better through the thick cloth of night, wishes that the moonlight and starlight shimmering on the ocean could be wiped away. She wants to see into the water. As it is, the vast depths are impenetrable. Beneath her could be a hundred sea monsters, a thousand gaping maws, an infinity of hungers and dangers and implacable unfeeling evils. Or there could be nothing. Blank, unforgiving emptiness, punctuated only by Betha herself and this clump of mystery.

She wants to get closer to the sea-not-weed, but starting her boat's motor might disturb the shape. She shifts her weight slightly so the skiff naturally turns towards the tendrils, keeping her eyes locked on them. They're a bit closer now, maybe twenty meters instead of thirty, but still hard to get a clear look at. Until they begin to rise from the water's surface.

In the moonlight it is difficult to make out color, but Betha can tell the tendrils are bright platinum, perfectly matching the platinum scales covering the siren's forehead. And as the beast gently rises slightly higher out the water, hardly making a ripple in the bobbing waves, ridges resembling eyebrows and a prominent nose and platinum round, scaled lips come into view. The impression is one of monochrome humanity, apart from the eyes. The eyes are set too far apart, much too far for beauty, and are perfectly round with reflective irises that shine with the same platinum shade. As the siren observes Betha, it turns its head to the side and peers down its elongated nose. A single pupil dilates to assess her. She must pass whatever test the siren has, because it begins to sing.

As her ears fill with noise, Betha reflects that perhaps the correct word would not be singing, but resonating. After all, the siren's mouth doesn't open. The sound emanates from just below the water's surface, where the siren's chest is. It is a saccharine, metallic ringing, punctuated by occasional staccato chimes. The tone reverberates across the gentle waves and burrows into Betha's head, rolling around the inside of her skull and vibrating in her jaw. It's a sound she imagines someone else could love, but to her ears it is a grating, deceitful drone, trying to convince her to be at rest, to trust it, when she will never be at peace again, not since Conor was taken from her. She hates buzzing, consuming sounds. They overwhelm her. Make her stomach turn. She covers her ears and focuses on the noise of the salt water lapping against the sides of the skiff. She can't turn back now, not when she's so close.

The siren cocks its head at Betha's lack of response. The ropey tendrils mimicking hair fall back, revealing that it lacks external ears and instead seems to have soft indentations, like a bruised apple. She can tell its shoulders move slightly underwater, the sound growing louder in concert with the movement, but the sound overwhelms Betha too much to attack. She remains still.

The noise finally cuts off when the creature slips underwater. Betha curses herself for not being able to act, but then it silently reappears, closer to the boat, only fifteen or so meters away now. She could probably get a good shot at it at this distance, but she only has the one spear loaded, the one chance. She needs to be sure. She needs it to be as close as possible.

"Right, so, here we are now," she softly coos, trying to let her brogue roll around in her lungs to mimic way the creature made its horrible sounds. It cocks its head to the other side, using its second eye to examine her.

"I assume you're hungry, you terrible beast," she murmurs as she slowly reaches for her rations. The siren jerks back warily, but Betha makes soothing humming sounds and it doesn't descend into the depths. She continues humming as she pulls aside the tarp and digs out a bit of dried jerky.

"We know you're a predator, don't we?" Betha purrs, tossing a small strip of meat as close to the siren as she can. The siren slides through the water to it, barely seeming to expend any effort to swim. When it is only a few inches away from the floating jerky, quick as a flash its mouth opens. Betha sees a second set of pharyngeal jaws appear at the back of its throat to grab the morsel.

"Disgusting," Betha murmurs sweetly. "You disgust me, you freak of nature."

She tosses more jerky into the water, nearer the boat this time, luring the creature closer, closer, ever closer. It is an arduous task. The creature frequently skitters away and reapproaches, but Betha is determined. Once she has it only two or three meters away, she's able to see it clearly. She was right about the platinum scales, the ridges, the fish eyes, and the hair resembling gummy jellyfish tentacles.

However, in that tentacle hair, she is surprised to see decoration: bits and bobs woven into and around the tendrils, clearly not part of the siren. She wonders, since it bothers to make itself up, if perhaps the creature is more human than it looks. Perhaps it would be immoral to kill it. She isn't even certain this is the one that killed Conor. She peers closely at the baubles and can make out a small sand dollar with a hole carved out of the middle, a shimmery fishing lure, a stiff blue starfish, and a golden band.

A thick golden band with an intricate claddagh stamped into the metal. Just the same as hers but bigger.

Betha's heart turns sour. There is no humanity in this abomination, there is only death and murder and cruelty. She takes a large chunk of jerky and tosses the meat to the siren. As the beast trustingly devours the meal, she hefts up the spear gun, steadies the heavy wooden stock against her body, and aims. She squeezes the trigger. The spear is unleashed.

When the blade lances through the siren's left clavicle, its narrow shoulders jerk back in agony. Its mouth opens and emits new sounds, sounds for its own kind rather than sounds meant to attract prey. Both sets of jaws open and snap in rapid succession, panicked but still in patterns recognizable as intricate and purposeful. The sharp clicks of its teeth travel across the open waves.

Betha grabs the rope that fixes the gun and the spear together and hauls, bunching the muscles that layer her back and shoulders together, dragging the monster to her boat. It tries to pull the spear from its shoulder, wrapping both of its three-digit, sharp-clawed hands around the shaft and pulling, but only serves to help Betha by hooking itself more completely. As Betha's pulls increase in tempo, it gives up on removing the spear. It thrashes instead. Betha's body jerks left and right, but she holds tight and drags the siren ever nearer.

When the siren is within arm's length of the skiff, still fighting against its inevitable doom, Betha grabs a fistful of its hair to drag it aboard. She drops it just as quickly, feeling lashing lines of burning pain cross her palm. Her guess that the siren's hair resembled jellyfish tentacles was more accurate than she had thought. The siren, noticing her faltering, takes its chance and dives deep, even as the spear still pierces it through.

"Jesus, Mary, and Joseph," Betha swears in frustration. The rope unspools, more and more of it disappearing deep into the frigid waters. She snatches as it slips away from her, nearly too late, only just catching it before the gun is ripped from her. As she tightens her hands around it, the stung palm screams through her nerve endings. Remaining steadfast, she locks the pain away in a different part of her mind, keeping hold and stopping the siren's escape. The skiff pitches perilously to one side as the siren swims ever-deeper, threatening to toss Betha overboard, but she leans backwards to redistribute her substantial body weight and the boat levels. Slowly, hand over burning hand, centimeter by centimeter, she drags the siren back from the depths into the warmer surface waters.

This time, when the thrashing siren bursts through, splashing salty water into Betha's mouth, she grabs directly for the spear. It held while she dragged the beast out of the bowels of the ocean. It will hold when she drags it onto the skiff.

She lifts it out of the sea. It is a long creature, maybe a meter and a half from tip to tail, and it's heavy, but not as heavy as a person, maybe only five stone or so. It is no match for Betha's six-foot height or her fifteen stone of rough-hewn strength.

It slices at her cheek with bony claws, ripping off the fake beard as well as some of her wrinkled flesh. Even as the blood pours from her face, Betha doesn't falter. She tosses the monster onto the boat, between her meager supplies and the small motor. Her heavy boot, pressing down on its scaled, writhing pelvis, holds it. As she takes her knife from its holster it gasps and, in desperation, moves its hands towards its chest.

Betha keeps her boot in place, crushing it slightly, but stops for long enough to see what it plans to do. It's then she notices a hollow bowl shape depressed into the creature's chest and stomach, with a hard ridge bordering it on all sides. The siren takes its right hand and extends the second claw, the one Betha thinks of as the pinky finger, and drags it around the rim of the recess. The sound resonates, quietly at first. Then increasing its ringing and rolling and droning tone until it is scraping again at the inside of Betha's tender braincase.

"Would you stop that?" she screams at it, collapsing her body onto the beast's chest to pin it in place under her, trapping the arm making the sound. "That God-awful racket!"

The ringing noise is abruptly cut off by the attack. The siren raises its one free arm up, making the palm flat in feeble defense and in supplication. Betha looks into its shallow, globular eyes as it clicks its two sets of jaws at her in distinctive, overlapping patterns. She positions the tip of her knife in between two of its ribs, near where its heart should be.

Its odd clicking jaws must be some form of rudimentary language. Maybe the thing can understand her, after all. "Are you begging for your life?" she softly whispers.

The siren's facial muscles grow slightly more expressive. If it were a person, Betha would've said it looked hopeful. It continues to click back at her in desperation.

"Did Conor beg for his?" Betha hisses, using both of her hands to plunge the knife into its platinum chest. She immediately wrenches the knife free, and punctures the creature's chest once more, for insurance. As awareness drains from its countenance, Betha rips the tendril Conor's wedding band is wrapped around out of the siren's scalp, ignoring the fresh burning stings as she works the ring off and slips it into her pocket. Very little blood pours from the creature's wounds. Fish don't bleed much, after all.

A few hours later, exhausted to her bones but peaceful in her heart, Betha and her tiny skiff approach the docks. A government boat, much grander than her own, drifts close to her. A short, mustached man aboard it pulls out a megaphone, asking her: "Do you have a fishing license?"

"Don't need one," she calls back. "Wasn't out fishing."

"Ma'am, with all due respect, I can see the fish on the back of your boat." He gestures to the large platinum tail behind Betha, poking out from under the tarp.

Betha pulls the tarp aside, showing the man the siren's womanly body, clawed arms, and dead, gelatinous eyes. His own eyes widen in disbelief.

Betha smirks. "It's not a fish, is it?"

LIVING DEATH BENEATH THE WAVES
H.V. Patterson

Men drifted past, eyes sliding over her and away. The air was dry and harsh on her skin, but she could not leave until she fulfilled her purpose. How she longed for the caressing weight of the ocean depths. She exhaled pheromones and waited.

* * *

Cheap wine coated Hal's gums, redolent of blood, rubbing alcohol, rust. He didn't know anyone at this mediocre gallery. But the stress of the divorce proceedings had hollowed him out, and he was an empty vessel craving nothing but distraction and alcohol. Anything would do, even cheap, cloying wine. As long as he didn't spend yet another evening alone.

He was older than most of the chic artists, buyers, and pretenders, and still wearing his three-piece suit. The suit, as always, felt like an ill-fitting disguise. He longed to tear everything off, starting with the bright red tie strangling him, and set it all ablaze. If he did, he might be applauded for convincing performance art: mid-life crisis, a symbolic burning away of this role he'd worn for twenty years. But who he was beneath the suit, he couldn't say.

And what did he have to show for all those years? A child he never saw, a dissatisfied wife, a cramped office, the knowledge that every day he grew more irrelevant, more out of touch with the engineers he supervised.

Hal gathered his courage and forced himself to move. He strode past a series of boorishly provocative photographs and chaotic assemblages abstracted beyond any meaning – to him, at least. Two people near him seemed to glean meaning from the manic splatters of red, gold, black, blue.

"It's the primordial sea, the chaos of life," the first enthused.

"You can see the artist's angst, how she used her art to work through postpartum depression," the second agreed. "Her celebration of the cruel willfulness of nature, its fundamental amorality, its lack of regard for us and our petty lives."

"Life is cruel. Nature wants us to reproduce, but beyond that, what does it care?"

The words rang like warning bells in Hal's head as he drifted to the back of the gallery. Stepping into this space felt like gliding from the crowded shallows to the murkier waters of the ocean. In this dim corner hung hyper-real paintings of strange fish, denizens of the abyssal zone, the dark depths sunlight never penetrates. He examined glowing jellies, giant isopods feasting on indeterminate bones, and a goblin shark, its improbable face turned toward him, dark eyes twinkling with secret knowledge.

The most striking painting was the anglerfish:

scaleless red-black skin covered in bumpy protrusions; gaping needle-teeth, too large for his mouth; lure suspended before him, a will-o'-the-wisp enticing fishes to their doom. The painting was at least ten feet long, bigger than any known anglerfish, every unlovely detail rendered with gorgeous clarity. It was so vivid Hal could almost imagine reaching through the canvas and pulling out a living creature.

When Hal was a child, he'd loved reading about the deep oceans, as inaccessible as the moon and less well-mapped than the lunar surface. He'd been captivated by the grainy images of alien creatures alive and thriving on earth.

He should take his daughter, Emily, to the aquarium soon. She was growing up, losing her childlike wonder. Not even eleven, and her eyes were too like his own: dark circles worn beneath them by the relentless waves of school, homework, and extracurricular activities.

He felt a bright flash of anger on Emily's behalf. Why were things the way they were, so much pressure with only fleeting flashes of pleasure to break up the monotony? And so many of those bright pleasures were lures, tempting you deeper and deeper into debt, into unwanted commitments, into a life you'd never planned. He'd been caught in the riptide, yanked from the bright shore of youthful aspirations. He didn't want that for Emily.

Life is cruel, he thought, *a series of pre-made choices, all leading to a leviathan, eager to devour you—*

"Do you like her?" said a sultry voice to his left.

Hal turned and beheld a woman who matched every feverish daydream her voice conjured. She wore a shimmering silver dress brimming with tasteful rhinestones. Her earrings and necklace were milky-black pearls. She stood close, intimately close, her neck yearning towards him, her eyes a green so dark they were almost opaque, her shining black hair flowing like an oil slick down her exposed neck and shoulders. Her mouth was the only thing about her that wasn't beautiful: her lips were wide and thin, painted red, lipstick cracking at the corners.

Her scent washed over Hal. He'd never smelled anything so intoxicating. He leaned closer, barely restraining himself from burying his face in her oil-slick hair. She smelled like salt and lilies and yearning.

"Her?" he forced himself to ask.

"That's a female," she said, nodding at the anglerfish.

"How do you know?"

"There are over two hundred known species of anglerfish," she said. "Their mating habits are...varied. In this particular species, only the females have the lure and grow to maturity."

"What about the males?" Hal asked.

Something pressed against his memory, as if he'd known the answer at one point. But the gulf between the boy he'd been and the man he was now was too vast.

"They're much smaller, but they have their uses," she said, smiling like a sphinx. "So, do you like the painting?"

"It makes me want to take my daughter to the

aquarium," Hal said. "I want to show her how much we still don't know, even about our own planet. I feel like everything she experiences is so mundane, like she's already bored of being alive, like she's already becoming…"

Hal trailed off, unable to say the last part: *as apathetic, as pathetic, as I am.*

He twisted the empty glass in his hands. Cheap plastic. He wondered how many cups from this gallery would end up in the ocean, break down into microplastic particles, and eventually enter the food chain, accumulating in some poor fish's living tissues.

The woman smiled, and his anxiety melted away as she pressed her cool hand over his restless fingers. Her teeth were too white and perfect to be real; they must be veneers.

"You have a daughter!" Her scent cocooned him in a drunken haze.

She glanced back at the painting, and something about the proprietary sweep of her eyes made him ask, "Are you the artist?"

She nodded.

"I'm glad my work makes you think of your daughter," she said. "What are we in the end without children? A broken link in an ancient chain, a permanent and irreparable severing between past and future." She leaned closer. Her voice tickled the edge of his ear. "Without children, we are but a wound which can never be healed, swallowed by deep time and forgotten."

Hal couldn't breathe. Her presence swam over him. Her bare arm and shoulder pressed against his suit jacket. Her hair was a fine net settling over his elbow. When he met her gaze, her pupils were swollen with promise.

Hal flirted, and she flirted back, accepting his compliments but offering nothing personal about herself, not even her name. He quickly grew enraptured. She gleamed like a pearl amongst the other artists. From their dark, secluded corner, everyone else looked like skittish fish in the waiting room of a mediocre doctor's office. All surface brilliance, no depth.

She asked him to leave with her, soft cheek pressed against his. Her cool fingers wrapped around his wrist, tugging him along with surprising strength. Hal stifled his guilt and doubts. His divorce was almost finalized. Besides, according to his wife Debbie, their marriage had been over for years.

They stepped into the night and the full moon greeted them. A salt-stained breeze ruffled their hair as she led them to nearby Land's Edge Beach. During the day, the beach teemed with swarms of tourists and locals. Now it was deserted. Hal's feet sank into the sand, and he stopped to fumble open his laces and pull off his socks and shoes. She kicked her thin, strappy heels off and tugged him towards the water.

Hal hesitated. He glanced over his shoulder, taking comfort in the harsh lights of nearby civilization. Emily's face flashed across his mind, but he refused to let guilt or shame pull him under. It was just one night on the beach with a beautiful woman. He deserved this much. He tried to ignore the coarse, irritating grains of sand scouring his uncalloused feet. He tried not to think about the sand fleas, bugs, and parasites milling in the sand. He let her lead him, step by step, to the water. Soon, wavelets rippled over their feet, licking at their toes.

"I don't even know your name," he said.

She smiled and removed her dress. She stepped deeper into the water, and Hal followed. His eyes fluttered shut as her scent settled over him. Her teeth caressed his vulnerable throat and nipped the shoreline of his lips, eroding all resistance.

He didn't break the kiss when her hands fumbled at his pants then his boxers, shucking them off. He didn't break the kiss when she stripped off his tie, jacket, and shirt, buttons ripping from their anchors. Her arms were bands of knotted muscle, crushing his naked body against hers, skin against skin. Her fingers tangled like seaweed in his hair, holding him steady when he stumbled and cut his foot on a fragment of shell. She sucked his small gasp of hurt into her mouth.

Hal finally broke the kiss, gasping for air. They were knee-deep in the ocean. She was gloriously naked, taller and more angular than she'd seemed in the gallery. Her eyes glowed with their own inner light as she tugged him deeper, water flowing up his thighs and over his pelvis. He turned and looked behind them, comforted to see the shore still close, the dark blots of their discarded clothes like bits of detritus washed ashore.

When Hal was a teenager, he'd often swum into the ocean from this very beach, lazily backstroking until the city skyline became a wavering mirage. He was so much older now, and he couldn't remember the last time he'd swum for more than a few minutes.

"Come with me," she said. "I want to make love to you in the water."

Before Debbie and Emily, Hal would've gone without a thought. He'd followed the beautiful woman this far, drunk off her smooth skin, her heady scent, her shining eyes.

But he saw Emily's face again, the naked hurt that flashed across it whenever he and Debbie fought over something inconsequential, like bills, taxes, whether they should continue eking out an existence on California's eroding coast or flee to the cheaper pastures of the Midwest. Maybe he and Debbie could talk to each other, really talk. It wouldn't stop the divorce, but they could clear the air. They both wanted the best for Emily, and things were so unstable now, both in their fragmenting family and in the wider world.

Or maybe the world has always been uncaring and cruel, he thought, *eager to devour the weak and sick, and I'm only now feeling the hot stink of its breath.*

"I'm sorry, I can't do this," Hal said.

He tried to step back, but the woman's fingers tightened around his wrist. She pulled him farther out to sea. The cold and hungry ocean settled over his shoulders, sprays of displaced saltwater nibbling his kiss-stung lips.

"What are you doing!" Hal spluttered, wiping salt from his eyes with his free hand.

The woman changed. Her thin mouth, wider than ever, stretched from ear to ear, displaying long, sharp teeth. Her hair was replaced by protruding dark growths. Her forehead bubbled and melted away, and a fleshy tendril topped with a bright, pulsating star uncurled from her skull.

Its blue-green glow soothed Hal's terror, lulling him into a waking dream. When she tugged his wrist again, he let her pull him farther out. Soon his feet no longer touched the seabed. Years of swimming lessons kicked in, and Hal instinctively tread water, gazing at the bewitching light, mind calm and empty. She pulled him farther and farther from shore, the blue-green light swaying between them, beckoning him on.

A violent swell of water swept over Hal. It poured into his eyes and nose, burning his sinus cavity, blurring his vision. He came up spluttering and looked wildly around. It was like waking from a dream into a nightmare. He was far from shore, and he wasn't alone. There was a webbed, clawed parody of a human hand wrapped implacably around his wrist. He looked up at the woman, and nothing of the beautiful artist remained in this monster's face. When she smiled, her distended mouth split her visage in half, revealing rows of needle-sharp teeth the color of smoky topaz, each as long as his spasming fingers. The light that emanated from her forehead, the hypnotic light that had led him without resistance to the open waters, protruded from a thick, ugly appendage in the center of her forehead; an anglerfish's lure.

Bioluminescent bacteria: that's what makes the glow, he remembered unhelpfully.

"Don't be afraid," she said.

Her voice was still low and beautiful, though there was a rumble beneath it, and she grimaced, like it was becoming difficult to speak. She continued to grow larger and less human, her features distorting, her eyes turning cold and alien.

Hal struggled, but it was useless. She seized his free hand with her clawed fin and dove beneath the surface. Hal swung his head up and back. He took a last, frantic look at the moon and the dark sky, a tapestry set with glimmering stars. He inhaled salt-tinged air just before she pulled him underwater.

Hal thrashed as they descended. The pressure of the ocean closed around him like a vise, threatening to collapse his burning lungs. His blood lurched through his skull, every heartbeat a frantic struggle. He avoided looking at her as he fought for his life, fearing the power of her lure. She must be a mermaid, some flesh-eating siren borrowing tricks from an anglerfish.

Just when Hal thought the pressure would break him, she stopped moving, her hands still anchored to his wrists. Despite himself, Hal beheld her. By the blue-green bioluminescence of her lure, he saw that she'd grown massive. He could only see part of her undulating torso, her powerful fins and tail. Her teeth were as long as his forearms, too big for her gaping mouth. They hung weightless in the smothering water, her lure glowing between them like a fallen star: man and monster locked together in the dark, cold waters.

Hal's oxygen-starved mind fired off useless thoughts and questions: *She could snap me into pieces so easily, break me against her cruel teeth. Does she always play with her food like some monstrous femme fatale? Will giant isopods feed on my bones, or will she swallow me whole?*

"Stop fighting," she said, voice rippling through the water. "Everything's going to be fine."

But it was a lie. Nothing would ever be fine again. Emily's face flashed behind Hal's eyes. She'd be asleep now. What did she dream about? Somehow, he'd never asked her. He didn't know a single one of his daughter's dreams.

"I've been waiting for someone like you," she continued, her lure swaying flirtatiously. Against his will, Hal's eyes followed it, darting back and forth like entranced fish. "My eggs will be ready soon, and my children need a father."

Terror flooded Hal's oxygen-starved mind. The wild need to flee pulsed through his veins. He struggled but couldn't break free. She drew him closer until he was only inches from the massive expanse of her torso. Her hands were bony fins edged with razor claws. They bit into his tender skin as he floundered uselessly against her. Static crept across his vision. He was going to drown.

Hal ran out of air. He surrendered to the inevitable, his arms and legs going limp as a doll's. He opened his mouth, ready for the tidal rush of death. But only a trickle of water passed his lips before the monster pressed his mouth against her chest.

Her skin was sleeker than he'd expected, warmer than the chilling water. Slime and salt met his lips, coated his tongue. Her skin gave against his teeth, and Hal's mouth, face, head, his entire upper body, slid through her yielding flesh. Slime and salt enveloped him, cocooning him in cloying darkness.

Hal's head cleared for a second, as oxygen flowed from her body into his. He was frozen, paralyzed, boneless. Her scent flooded his mind, sending false signals of comfort singing down his synapses as he floated through a fog of something like love—a heady mixture of oxytocin and opioids.

"Relax." Her voice flooded through him, ringing through his faltering ears.

She swam down, propelled through the water by her powerful body. He could feel his legs and lower torso still outside of her body, drifting back and forth in the current, but he couldn't move. He couldn't even twitch a toe.

Hal's head and arms tingled. It was a strange sensation, not unpleasant or painful. His puny heart stuttered and went still as her circulatory system overwhelmed and integrated his, her heartbeat superseding his. His body wasn't his own anymore; it was transforming into an extension of her.

In Hal's dying brain, thoughts skittered and expanded, flowing in strange directions. Memories that weren't his slid through his mind, mingling and blurring the boundary between himself and the monster. Memories of water and darkness, of the tender flesh of fishes, whales, squid sliding down her voracious throat. Instincts deeper than hunger, propelling her to the surface, into an unfamiliar, clumsy form.

What is this? he thought.

In answer, one of his own long-buried memories uncoiled; a passage in a book accompanied by a picture which had left his childhood self amazed and appalled in equal measure. Some species of deep-sea anglerfish practiced sexual parasitism. Only the female grew to full maturity while the male remained much smaller and weaker. And once the female was ready to lay her eggs, she'd use pheromones to lure a male to her. He'd bite her, his jaw and body fusing into hers, transforming him into a sack of gametes, ever ready to fertilize her eggs.

You were never going to eat me, he thought. *You'd never go to such trouble for a meal.*

"You'll be the father to our children." Her whisper swam through his spiraling thoughts. "Our daughters."

Horror and revulsion struggled through the pleasant fog. Unmoving, unseeing, his heartbeat no longer his own, Hal tried to fight, to hold on to himself.

"Don't fight," she soothed. "You already have a human daughter on shore, and soon you'll have hundreds of daughters beneath the waves. You're fulfilling your biological purpose."

Hal was coming undone. His mind unraveled as her body absorbed the parts of him she didn't need. It was like slipping into a warm bath, like drifting into sleep, like being rocked in the cradle.

But there would be no return from this comforting darkness.

"Go to sleep," she said.

Emily's face drifted before him like an apparition, soft eyes filled with unconditional love. He tried to hold on, but her image faded away, as inaccessible as the depths of the ocean. The last of Hal's selfhood dissolved with his brain, digested by hungry cells. The mother-to-be would make good use of what remained.

* * *

She gave herself no name because she needed none. All predatory instinct, she dove homeward, down, down into the abyssal depths. Soon, she would lay her eggs. Soon, they would hatch. Hundreds of hungry daughters who would, in their turn, find mates and birth daughters, living links in an enduring, ancient chain.

UNCHARTED
JP Relph

There are more human remains in the ocean than in all the terrestrial graveyards combined.

Coraline

When I drowned, the sky above was deepest blue, sequinned with stars. I had one last thought before the ocean's embrace, tight as a yearning lover's, smothered me to velvet cold: a memory of a sparkling dress worn at a Christmas party, with red shoes. Shocking red shoes with killer heels. I'd chosen them to take the attention from my face, from the smile doing little to embellish the hollowness that was always revealed by my eyes.

I'd chosen them to hide behind. I don't even like red. I hated Christmas. In the end I hated everything—especially myself.

By walking into the ocean, pockets filled with returning pebbles, I hoped that hollowness would be forever filled with cleansing saltwater. As I was conveyed to uncharted depths, the stars vanished from my sight like summer freckles in winter.

* * *

When I woke, the water around and above me

shimmered with preternatural light. I stared at my hands, turning them over and over, shocked by how they flickered from solid to translucent, allowing small curious fish to slip through my palms before becoming corporeal again. I spun in the water like a jellyfish. What had I become? Was this what death looked like? I felt the ocean surge through my body, warm like blood, yet I couldn't feel my heart. Its shattered beat had been all I'd known once. Its absence was oddly comforting.

* * *

I drifted through currents, finding a grace and ease of movement. Crustaceans and sea-flora became enwoven in my hair. I was never completely alone. I pushed myself to the ocean's bed, the exquisite midnight-blue, where satiny covers puffed with the tossing and turning of restless bedfellows. I burrowed into the sand like an eel, curled and closed my eyes. I had given myself to the ocean—she had brought me back. I still didn't know why. Yet in this strange form, purged and remade by seawater, I'd found a peace long denied me. I rested.

* * *

There's no consideration for time in the deep ocean. I swim and I rest. I never surface in daylight – thoughts of the sun's revealing glare repel me. I am of the salty darkness now. A darkness teeming with colour. Months may have passed, longer; it doesn't concern me. I'm untethered in this subaquatic world—freed from physical pains and emotional torments. I know the ocean wants something from me in return. I still wait for my salt-burned eyes to show me the way.

* * *

I skim the ocean floor, stirring sand with my fingers. In the glimmering green-gold, something incongruous is unveiled: a tragic human form, female, scraps of sea-bleached cloth clinging to white bones. Scorpion fish whip strands of silver hair around the skull, as if they wish to plait it. Tabby cat mackerel brush against two hands grasping upwards like pallid crabs. Threads of faded-blue rope trail from her wrists. I look down, see the same knotted at the ankles. As the sands shift further, I see rocks beneath her pelvis—grey, not of this place. This isn't someone who gave herself to the ocean as I did. She was discarded here. She doesn't belong.

When I rise, the cuckoo rays whirl a funnel to carry the woman, freed from a sandy grave, up, up, up. I push her into the shallows, the cover of night hiding our grim purpose. The ocean sighs, waves shiver, roll her gently onto the beach.

I stare a while at the lonely bones, luminescent in the moonlight. I hope she is soon discovered, named, rested in a terrestrial grave-bed. Perhaps visited by loved ones with tear-spattered roses and lilies. For a selfish moment I want to crawl up beside her, feel the cold press of stones and shells on my knees, the piquant wind on my lips. But I do belong to the ocean. Weighted with a purpose unknown in life. A duty. I turn my face from dawn's goldening promise, follow trails of bramble sharks down, down, down.

* * *

The ocean continues to unveil the lost. With each sand-softened bone, each circlet of blue threads around a fragile joint, rage thrashes inside me, builds like a tidal wave. I can do nothing but let it wash over the beach, bearing the wretched dead. Hope their discovery will lead someone to the door of an earthbound beast. While my salt-blood burns with the urge to lead the beast here, to the anguish of the ocean. To me.

* * *

Susannah

You should have trusted that twisting in your gut, the prickle that raced like hot gooseflesh over your skin. He was all wrong. You smelled it, tasted it somehow in the air around him. You felt it when his eyes, pond-scum green, abandoned his practised smile. You should have lashed out, screamed, run. You can't now. You can only close your eyes, find a memory to hide in, away from his clammy hands on you, the fried-fish stink of his breath.

Summer heat still baking the sand. Laughter bright as the fairy lights strung between poles. An unexplored swirl of glowing skin; sweat and coconut. Eyes so blue they must have drained the morning sky. Her kiss all grapefruit lip balm and hot need. The beach has blurred—you only see her, feel her. Her hands on the pale skin beneath your bikini, scorching like the sun. Cora. Your greatest love. Your greatest loss. Your mind clings to that pecan skin, those beautiful eyes. She wasn't haunted then. She was wild and free as the ocean.

You're yanked hard from that summer haze into stinging cold air. The same ocean, but darker, uglier, horribly close. It seems to whisper your name in susurrant urgency. You fill your eyes with stars, let tears full of light spill over. You barely feel the tightening of ropes, the gouging bite. You let the shush of the waves mask his ugly breathing; fetid and fevered.

When the hard slap of water comes, a numbness spreads over the pain, blanketing. You're falling through layers of deepening blue, a fist of ice in your chest. In the final moments, your mind conjures grapefruit kisses and a love blistering as an August sun. Wild and free.

* * *

Tierney

He watches the melee from atop the cliff, pressed against his car window like a fretful dog. Rainclouds mask the sun, fill the car with cold shadows. The news told of a twelfth body spewed onto the beach, laid out on the stony sand like rattling flotsam. They might identify this one—six others had been named so far—finally find the common thread. A tenuous, fraying connection between the victims. Between them and him. Red strings on a corkboard.

The car has gotten stuffy, sour from his sweat and breath. He swipes the window clear with a sleeve. Below, the beach is clearing, no more to be mined from the pebbled sand. A green tent collapsed. A trail of black and yellow tape snaps in the wind as it's rolled up. He stares at the ocean, its mocking calm. His hands tighten around the steering wheel, turning white as the beach-belched bones. Why is this happening? How? He's shrewd, cautious with his work. There were no markers to lead to graves, certainly no trophies—his deeds left intentionally unmapped. He sent them all to the ocean floor with rocks and ropes. Their remains should have been scattered and scoured, buried by the sands. Lost.

It was if they'd found wilful purpose, driven by a desire for reckoning. His chosen ones returning, in more than just his dreams. Impossibly pushing their fleshless arms through the water, their skulls breaching the frothing surface. Their disarticulated skeletons clatter-clambering onto the pebbles, waiting to be found by fishermen and beach-combers. Waiting to be named. To name him.

His frustration sours to foreboding, like clotting milk, making him retch. It's a wholly unfamiliar sensation. He can't bear the way it squirms in his belly like elvers, weakening him. In the mirror, he seeks his own eyes, then lurches from what now cowers there, whimpering in the muddy green. The urge to take another now shivers impotently beneath a pressing dread, won't be prised free. Is he broken? Lost?

* * *

He can't fathom what possesses him to leave the car, descend to the beach—the very place of his unravelling. The pebbles, cleared of accusatory bones, are silvered and pearled by a sharp moon. He feels lured here, as if tempted by a blood-red apple, a blood-red kiss, tainted by salt. In a way, he believes that by returning to the churn and chop of the ocean, he'll learn why it schemes against him.

It's a mild night, he's weary, sweat-sour, and the shushing water is a dark temptation. He kicks off his shoes, presses his toes into the yielding sand. He closes his eyes, remembers the last time he felt that cold squelch.

Winter-white skin; silky as the heart of shells, limpid brown eyes; diamond tears quivering on lashes, blue rope parting under his blade with a sound like sensual breath.

When he fails to become aroused at the memory, he realises the breadth of his anxiety. He remains flaccid. Letting out a cry, mournful as a seabird, he wades into the wavelets, watches them break like pale necks where they impact his shins. The water tugs at his ankles, then his calves. He imagines it is another of his chosen ones, returned to him, trying to snag him with a fleshless hand. He isn't soothed by the chill water, nor the expanse of star-filled sky, he feels only a gnawing inside him, a devouring. Anxiety becomes fear. He's rocked by it.

Then he's yanked hard, a sensation like claws digging into his flesh, and dragged to deeper water. He rolls and thrashes like a crocodile, coughing, choking on vile froth. He tries to swim, grabbing at the water with numbing arms. He tries kicking. He has no strength; he's truly flaccid. The grip is relentless, like rope around his ankles. Then his thighs. Screaming only invites frigid brine into his body. An excruciating pain, like boiling vinegar in his lungs. Spent and fully submerged, he sees terrifying dogfish circling like subaquatic vultures, snapping with needle-teeth. A black certainty intrudes on his consciousness—he's drowning. Even in a semi-delirious state he sees the irony in that.

As he claws at the last residues of air, the dogfish bolt away and, in their place, madness comes. For surely the diaphanous woman appearing before him is a hallucination, an artefact of his diminishing brain. Yet she seems unbearably real. Something in the furious glare of her blue eyes, like impossible gas flames. He feels his own eyes crackle, shatter. A brutal shiver of sharks grin eagerly behind the woman, promise that drowning will merely be part of his torment.

This is to be his sentence, delivered by this judge of the ocean: a woman in washed-denim robes, a wig of brown and green crowned in shells. A delicate plaited bracelet of faded-blue strings encircles her wrist. She smiles like a beautiful monster, drifts aside to present him to the executioners. When he hears her speak, her voice is so cruel in its whispery kindness:

"You belong here."

Then she's spinning away and retribution comes fully, with teeth ripping and bones snapping, and he knows there'll be nothing left to wash ashore.

* * *

Coraline

I swim and I rest. I never surface during daylight. I am of the salty darkness now. A darkness teeming with colour. I sometimes rise to look at the sky when it's sequinned with stars. Months pass, longer. Then a shoal of tabby cat mackerel whips aside a blanket of sand, reveals what slumbers beneath.

    I run my fingers across the skull, feel the smooth hole. He doesn't belong here. My duty is to give him the peace he's been denied. The justice. I summon the cuckoo rays and together we take him up, up, up.

AQUA WARRIOR WITCHES SAVE OUR WATER!
Alicia Hilton

Some aqua warrior witches experience epiphany
canoeing on lakes, bodysurfing on seas,
new views on peace, justice, and ecology.

Others find fulfillment casting hexes
on whalers so they drown in the deep dark drink
predator versus predator, eco-warrior supremacy.

Some aqua warrior witches hunting for flesh
only devour scallops, abalone, and squid
because the taste of humans makes them retch.

Others hunt scumbags who toss plastic in oceans
guzzle their blood with gusto, even swallowing
bluebottle flies wriggling on polluters' legs.

Some aqua warrior witches born with a best before date
stamped on both their feet would burn their soles,
hoping sizzled skin would change their fate.

Others advertise their upcoming downfall,
sell tickets to benefit Greenpeace, not knowing if
they will wake needing a heart transplant or dialysis.

What if you woke with your death date
written in squid ink across your chest
would you kill for clean water?

SAVE FOR JOY
Noah Lloyd

Bubbles form in the guts of the mushroom soup, rise, and spill their vapor into the warm galley. Rob hefts the huge stock pot from the stove—even with tightly woven oven mitts over his hands, he feels the heat coming off the pot's handles. The pot is heavier than he expected. A wave rolls beneath the ship at right angles to the beam, rocking them sharply side to side. They may be at anchor, but that means little to the sea.

I should have left it on the damn stove, Rob manages to think before the boiling liquid goes everywhere, drenching his face and arms and chest, surely blistering and badly burning him.

Rob isn't even supposed to be here. Maybe if he was a better seaman, maybe if he ever got those sea legs everyone talked about, but he's too damn clumsy.

But the soup doesn't go everywhere—instead he somehow braces his feet against opposite walls of the tiny kitchen in a panicked split, the soup sloshing dangerously before calming down in the pot, which is still in his hands. In its cradle, the stove rocks forward and back, designed to prevent exactly the kind of accident Rob nearly experienced, even in rough seas.

Dodged that one, he thinks.

It's Final Night. Tomorrow, they'll sail back

up the Strait of Juan de Fuca and the passengers will disembark in Seattle, and Rob will be out of a job again.

A stack of metal bowls clatters onto the counter next to the stove. On most nights, the passengers eat off of fancy ceramicware and drink from crystal glasses, but on Final Night the passengers and crew eat together. The meal is always simple ***sailors fare***, as the brochure advertises, missing the apostrophe. It is the last of a six-night voyage.

Rob isn't supposed to be here, he reminds himself as he bears the pot up the stairs from the galley at the back of the ship, the *Kohekohe*, registered in New Zealand though it's never seen the islands even from a distance. She is a 105-foot schooner, which means two masts, fore and aft, hung with pearl-white sails that the company makes sure are cleaned between every voyage. A little excessive, but they shine in tourists' photos.

The pot heavy in his arms, Rob sees a long table formed by loose planks balanced on overturned milk crates. The table runs the length of the deck between the foremast and mainmast, and the passengers and crew sit on cushions, legs crossed, or legs tucked under them, or out to the side, some of the female passengers' skirts bundled around their knees.

They are just *the passengers* to Rob and most of the crew. It is a joke among the crew—but only because it is true—that when a crewmate learns the name of a passenger, it means they have started sleeping together.

Seventeen people sit along the long running

table, twelve passengers and five crew. One of the crewmates—Catherine, the *Kohekohe*'s bosun—jumps up and helps Rob distribute bowls, helps him ladle the soup. Rob is the last to sit.

A long pause stretches out across the table. They all wait for Captain Clover, a gruff strip of dried leather, to say something, like acolytes waiting for their prophet to bless their meal. Finally, he clears his throat and mutters a few words of thanks for the guests sharing their company with the crew ("And their wallets," someone at the table mutters, but it gets a laugh from everyone, and the tension finally breaks).

Rob sits next to a cute curly haired passenger dressed in a white linen shirt. The passenger smiles at Rob one of those questing, uncertain smiles that invites him to talk. When Rob ignores the smile, the passenger turns to speak to the woman next to him. Rob eats his mushrooms in silence.

As they set to their victuals, deep below the *Kohekohe*, under two miles of water, something in the belly of the Earth shakes loose. A layer of frangible sedimentary rock shudders under a millennial pressure before finally cracking open, giving way to emission, a pocket of ethylene gas and hydrocarbons that stick together like a balloon as the whole rises toward the surface, taking its time, toward the *Kohekohe*.

Perhaps it is simply coincidence that their ship has dropped her sea anchor here, out of the entire, vast Pacific Ocean, or perhaps it is fate.

Rob is the only one belowdecks, with the dishes. While everyone else is above, drinking rosé, he rinses bowls and upturns them onto a white, rubberized drying rack. He isn't even supposed to be here. He thinks of Michael, alone in their apartment in New York, a continent-and-then-some away. Michael hadn't understood when Rob said that he was going back to cooking on a boat somewhere, or why that somewhere was off the Washington coast. Rob had a good job at the restaurant, and Michael needed him there, by his side, for all the appointments and the checkups, now more than ever.

"I'm sorry," Rob said then, and he says it again now.

Tomorrow he will be out of a job again, and he will have to decide if he'll go back to New York, back to the restaurants and the summer humidity and the hospital.

Maybe he'll go to Port Townsend. There's a boatbuilding school there, they'll know of other vessels in need of a cook.

Only a dozen feet below the *Kohekohe*, the balloon breaks apart into thousands of tiny bubbles, completing their journeys to the surface alone. If anyone looked overboard, they would have seen the *Kohekohe* sitting atop a boiling ocean, but no one witnesses the phenomenon, and then it is gone, filling the air with a poison lighter than water but heavier than air, which settles over them like an invisible cloudbank.

When Rob climbs back on deck after finishing the dishes, he's caught by a vision of the Washington shoreline, covered in trees, glimmering in their fall colors, gold and orange. The summer sun in this latitude is still an hour from setting, and it makes the shore look like fire. But the Washington coast should be covered in evergreens, and the *Kohekohe* is miles from shore.

There is no shore there, only water. The mirage passes as quickly as the certainty of the sight had hit him, and the certainty fades as fast.

Rob shakes his head, decides he needs a drink. Stepping over the limbs of passengers who have splayed out across the ship in a delicious relaxation, he looks for a glass and a not-empty bottle. As is unofficial and unprofessional custom, the crew has begun to socialize, learning the passengers' names.

The captain, with his wiry beard, chats with a woman with long black dreads who might be half his age. She says something and he laughs, his broken teeth yellow from tobacco.

Catherine lies across a large burlap sack full of Rob forgets what. Two men stand next to her, leering hungrily: her hand rests on one of their groins while she stares into the other's face.

Rob rubs his eyes. His head feels muddied, full, like an octopus unscrewed his skull and wants to climb inside. Come to think of it, as he looks back to the crew and the passengers, whose laughter he now registers as too high, off kilter, out of sync; it does seem like they are pairing off more blatantly, more shamelessly and publicly, than usual.

He thinks of the curly haired passenger. Doesn't see him on the deck. He thinks of Michael.

Something is terribly wrong. *But what is it?* Rob has trouble focusing. If he could only think straight for a second he might get it, might be able to stop whatever it is that's begun. Laughing, one of the younger passengers, some sixteen-year-old kid dragged along by his parents, lurches toward the foresheet, begins untying it.

Rob may be clumsy, and he may have been away from tallships for the past ten years, and his mind may be playing tricks on him, but even he knows that the wind is in the wrong direction for the kid to be doing what he's doing.

"Hey!" Rob shouts, moving forward.

But it's too late—the foresheet comes loose all at once, the lines pull through the block and the foremast's boom thunders free from where it had locked. Even with the foresail down and tied, the boom swings with a vengeance, connecting with the kid's head like a batter hitting a home run.

Crack.

The kid goes down just as Rob reaches him. His forehead is split open, blood pouring over one eye and onto the deck. Rob puts his hands on the boy's shoulders, neck, the side of his face, uselessly feeling for some sign of what he should do. The kid's eyes roll up white, and with hands shaking like a palsied old man the kid squeezes the sides of his own skull, trying to hold himself together, and moans.

Rob can feel the boom still swinging back and forth above him, looking for another target. "Help!" he shouts, looking fore and aft, for someone, the boy's parents, anyone to take this responsibility from him.

And then he sees Philippe—Thai-American, some French in his background, a drifter hired on to maintain their diesel engine this trip, but that doesn't matter because Philippe is toying with an emergency flare, playacting some G.I. from World War II or Vietnam for a fat Canadian woman, who laughs at him.

Maybe it's because Rob was belowdecks, the enclosure protecting him as the gas pocket leaked from the ocean like alcohol boiled out of wine, or maybe he simply has some kind of genetic protection that delays its effects, but he is the only one who can tell that something is wrong.

Philippe, his face a slackened and loose smile, shouts "Bang!" and fires the flare into the rigging, which ignites.

The passengers and crew all cheer and applaud, their faces lighting up by the glow of the flames like children under fireworks.

"Jesus Christ," Rob says, terror roosting in his stomach.

Keeping hunched beneath the boom and careful not to slip in the boy's blood, Rob grabs the kid by the shoulders of his shirt and drags him to the first of two lifeboats. The boy has given up trying to hold his head together. Rob lets go of him to unsnap the fasteners that keep the canvas cover spread across the lifeboat top like a drum, to keep the rain out. He went to the lifeboats automatically, years of life aboard ship, before settling in New York, coming back. Because the motions are automatic—from a thousand drills and one real emergency off Nantucket—it takes him a moment, too many moments, to realize that, still, no one has come to assist him.

Dread overtakes his terror, making a nest of his insides. He only gets halfway through unsnapping the fasteners. He can't look over his shoulder, for he knows that bacchanal and delirium are all that await him. Instead he looks out to sea. He must be facing east, for the sun is nowhere visible, and stars are creeping out to watch the end of the *Kohekohe*. But the stars are creeping *up* from the ocean. A reflection, Rob tells himself, a reflection a reflection, over and over, but it is not a reflection, and he cannot convince himself that it is. There are universes there in the ocean. Planets and quasars and nebulae in impossible colors that would break the world, and the emptiness between stars. The colors rise from the ocean like great, billowing curtains drawn across the sky.

Perhaps it is not the gas at all, but the mushrooms. Perhaps the farmer Rob purchased them from in Pike's Place Market knew they were corrupted, were no ordinary shiitake, had been harvested from a foul ground. Or there may have been a single *Psilocybe azurescens* accidentally included in the wild-caught mix, spoiling the whole pot.

Or perhaps the mushrooms were fine, but mixed with the gases of the deep ocean produced something new and unwholesome in the human body.

Or perhaps it is none of these, perhaps it is something far baser and grander.

Because the beauty of the night sky infecting the ocean is too great for him to stare at any longer, Rob turns back to the ship.

At the helm, the Canadian woman laughs while Philippe manhandles her. Clover has lifted his dreadlocked beauty by the thighs and presses himself between her legs, and her against the mainmast, and her mouth opens in pleasure. And Catherine, Catherine is on her knees with both men.

I'm not supposed to be here, Rob remembers,

the guilt and shame making his face hot (or are those the flames?). Rob sees Michael naked, standing in their living room in New York, blood running from an open sore in his hip, draining over his knee and pooling between his toes. Is it a memory or a vision? Rob can no longer tell. And if a vision, of the present or the future?

With his back to the oceanic stars, Rob takes in the kaleidoscopic colors that flicker above the ship. Across the still-solid deck, he makes eye contact with the curly haired passenger. The passenger's hair has become the woody stems of maple leaves turned gold and red in the fall. Scraps of the burning rigging that drift toward the deck are leaves falling from trees.

The curly haired passenger's skin has flaked and cracked, he is the leaves of a dry fall in upstate New York, a pile of them, ready to blow away, to fall inside of.

The ship unstitches itself beneath Rob's feet. Planks pull away from one another, their seams stretching until the tar caulking splits. The planks stand upright, like the trees they once were, the flatness of a timberboard giving way to roundness, giving way to the memory of bark and sap-flourishing branches. The ship is a forest, the sails a tattered canopy of orange and yellow twisting in a late-September sun, the mainmast but the tallest oak in this corner of a stretching wood.

Rob walks a path he remembers through the trees, the earth beneath his feet soft, a loam of decaying leaves and moss and living things, and it is the day he and Michael made love for, if not the first time, the best time.

As the curly haired passenger crumbles in the breeze, a raked-together leaf pile coming apart in a squall, Rob sees Michael again. They are together, maybe it is the first time, or the last time. Rob undresses Michael, there in the soft sunlight, removing his leather jacket and unbuttoning his jeans. They breathe quicker, both for the nearness of their skin and for the danger of their public indiscretion. They might be caught, they might be seen, but for now they do not care, the sun warms them despite the chill wind raising goosebumps across Rob's back and ass. And their nearness warms them, Michael's body like sunlight to Rob's cold hands.

There is no shore, nor no other ships to witness the madness aboard the *Kohekohe*, the riot of joy and sensation taken hold of its passengers, for they are all passengers now, who voyage, each, into memory, or into prophecy, for prophecy is but memory laid orthogonal to reality. Nor is there a witness to the *Kohekohe* as it lists to starboard, takes on water, flames spreading across her flanks, and begins to founder. There are no screams as the bulwarks and deck—a deck retaining something of its former life as forest—slip below the hallucinating waves, and the masts and yellow-orange sails plunge away forever. No screams save for those raised in joy.

A VOID, SUSPENDED WITH THAT WHICH CANNOT BE STARS
Taliesin Neith

What follows are select computer logs recovered from the black box of the Mitar. The Mitar was, according to the data, an unregistered MSV (Manned Submarine Vehicle) with an unknown occupant identifying themselves in the log as the captain. The black box was captured by an automated deep-sea trawler and recovered upon human inspection of anomalous objects in the hull. This unknown captain was seeking the Lilly Nora, a cruise liner in 2043 that capsized with all souls aboard lost. We hope that with the location data recovered that one day her grave will be found.

#LOG 983

Pressure failure in the cabin today. Luck saw it began moments after complete submersion; I was able to coax the Mitar to the surface and fling open the emergency hatch, and once I was certain I would not die so soon this morning, I climbed back in. Sitting in that metal box with sweat running down my spine already—it makes a woman's heart fail to see all alerts turn red and hear them start screaming. The AI was running resolution protocols from the moment the alarms began, but there was nothing. I will sit at the surface to-night, to stabilize the Mitar and set her to rights, but tomorrow I will take us down to start hunting for the Lilly Nora.

#LOG 984

I cannot risk another catastrophic failure once I am at the bottom of this ocean. Nor can I wait any longer to go down. It has taken longer than I desired to trace the error—a faulty wire feeding into all the sensors, a bridge between the AI and the rest of the Mitar. No wonder all the alarms went off; no wonder no resolution protocols worked, when the AI could not read any of the systems no matter how fast it rebooted and repaired them.

    I will have to be confident that a single faulty wire is all it was. Any longer and my present streak of good fortune will dim, and any competition will get closer to the wreck's location. Everything in my future rides on being the first to scavenge. That is how animals survive in the wild. We who arrive early gorge on the fat and the flesh, the organ meat, the blood. Those who arrive late will only have scraps left on the bones, and it is not always worth the risk.

#LOG 985

The descent begins. We go to her, the Lilly Nora, the white whale of any pirate worth their salt. I have calculated all the knowledge I can about her. She was carrying 5,982 souls when she disappeared. A hundred years and no trace. I believe I can find her.

She calls to me. At least, the tug behind my navel to search feels like her. Lilly Nora has said it is time to be found. I have calculated her approximate location based on the last exchange between the captain and a radio broadcaster warning of severe weather. Storms in the area have not abated in the past hundred years. I begin my descent outside their reach, in calmer waters. Cruise liners bigger than the Lilly Nora have sunk in the intervening decades, but they have all been found. Not her.

Of course, I am not working with knowledge nobody else has. I am following a call, a queer feeling in my gut. What I have, that many do not, is a scavenger submarine capable of reaching the ocean floor at fathoms untold. That is my advantage. I accept the incompleteness of my information and go forward.

She hides, but not from me.

#LOG 986

Descent in progress for two hours now. Mitar equipped with enough oxygen and fuel for two months. Pressurisation holding good and steady. Sun is long gone. The way it disappears captivates me. It dwindles. Not a setting, but all light is being drained from the world. It has been extinguished underwater.

Conserving energy until I reach the sea floor. Only necessary life support systems working. Horizontal thrusters powered by the Mitar's AI adjust its position to prevent us from drifting. Grabbers powered down, lights off save for this screen. I can see nothing outside my porthole. It is warm in here; I am stripped to the waist.

Every diver trying to impress a girl says that being this far down in a scavenger sub feels like being in a womb. He is usually trying to convince her of something, but that is beside the point: I do not disagree, in principle. The metaphor inspires life, but I have always felt more inclined to describe it as a coffin. There is death outside this capsule, a vacuum not made for humans: water in place of dirt, fish in place of worms.

Though the ocean floor has worms, too.

#LOG 994

Had a nightmare about pressure failure. I have always treated this log as a kind of dream diary. It is something for me to talk to. I sit in the cradle of the Mitar, typing into the computer, and I hope purging thoughts from my head will rid me of them. Here is what would happen to me if the Mitar failed, 6000 fathoms down: if there is damage to the vessel, the occupant may be immediately forced through whatever wound the Mitar (or other MSV) now has. My organs, all of them, will be sucked out and flung about, freed from the constraints of gravity and their role in my flesh-sack, now torn violently open. Parts of me may remain close by, but this will be incidental. Others will be carried away from the MSV by the currents, by passing creatures, by fate.

If the occupant—if I–am lucky enough to not be immediately and grievously mutilated in this fashion, my blood and saliva would boil. If I tried to hold my breath my lungs might explode inside of me.

A reprieve is that this would be very quick, although nobody has survived explosive decompression to tell the tale or relate to its quickness. It could be agonising, the awareness. This was the face of my nightmare. I felt my whole body come undone a piece at a time, and there was nothing I could do to stop it. I could only watch, from both within and without.

Here, affirmations: the cabin is pressurised with a good strong tank of oxygen, and I have been scavenging solo for many years now. The cabin can easily withstand these depths. This is an old submarine, well beyond her prescribed age of use, but she is sturdy. I have never known a problem I cannot repair.

#LOG 995

The submarine is creaking. I cannot sleep. I shall type until I nod off, I think. I ought to talk about things other than depressurisation. The Mitar is a single-person vessel. I stole her from a man who was not making best use of her. She has a patchwork leather steering chair that can be flattened out for sleeping. I have tins for pissing and shitting in. The rations I eat are life-preserving and designed to minimise bowel movements anyway—small and hard things with proteins, reminiscent of the pellets owls shit out. I am sweaty all the time. The Mitar is not wide enough for me to stretch my arms out across it—if I try my palms will press against old metal patches and welds, the monitors of the AI. It is hard to even be lonely here; you are so one and crowded by yourself. That said, it is a singular experience to masturbate at the bottom of the ocean. I am nestled there now, taking a break in the early days of this pursuit whilst I can. Letting the Mitar rest, almost entirely powered down, weighted against the nameless silt of the ocean floor, mankind's last unttttttttttttttttttt

I fell asleep on the keyboard. Signing off.

#LOG 1002

The ocean floor is not nameless. For so many it is home. It is just not mankind's home. I turned on the lights today to watch the bottom-feeders and strange eyeless creatures skim past. Shrimp are plentiful, and creatures so small that you cannot discern them from floating silt.

And I came upon a whalefall.

The sonar notified me of something large, potentially organic, and I went out of curiosity rather than need. The whale was recognisable by the size of it, and the knowledge that the Architeuthis dux has not enough bones to settle in this way. It had clearly sunk and died some months ago, the shape of it queerly contorted, bones spreading out as bottom-feeders disturbed them.

The whale was dead, but it was the most life I had ever seen. Pure life, not simply eating but thriving in amongst the bones. There were sticky, stringy bits of blubber clinging to the skeletal ribs and around and within it strange colourful plants spreading like moss—algae, I suppose, perhaps bacteria. The lights caught so much eyeshine, creatures that were predatory or frightened and blind, milky eyes unbothered by the glare. They hid among the bones.

Chased one another, ate one another, drifted, and explored and slept.

They lived in the corpse and made it theirs. A cathedral of the deep, the doors always open.

#LOG 1013

Lost a day tending to all systems. Had a strange turn. I became convinced I saw the Lilly Nora in the distance. All lights were off. I switched them on and saw nothing. I moved position forward and saw nothing.

. . .Hallucinations are not uncommon this deep. Sleep disruption, heat, lack of light. . .I have had them before. Pleased it was not oxygen leak and/or systems failure.

#LOG 1015

Sonar not enough today. Turned on all systems to use fully manual navigation. This is a good sign. I am deeper and closer. Too many obstacles for the Mitar's AI to calculate its own route. Seen more fish in the headlamps. Visibility is a losing game. There are rocks, passers-by, and beyond them only endless void, filled and suspended with that which cannot be stars. There is nowhere safe to bed down. I cannot risk leaving the Mitar running suspended in one spot, doing nothing whilst I sleep. All systems would fry. Better that I am the one to fry. I will forego sleep if possible. I know I am closer. I know I am.

#LOG 1023

Mitar is detecting significant sonar anomaly as we speak. I am asking the AI for further details... anomaly of around 400m/1312ft in length. The Lilly Nora was 365m/1198ft. This is within limits. Allows for the lack of precision in the Mitar's instruments, for drift, disruption, etc. Perhaps the Lilly Nora was significantly damaged. I would be more surprised if she were not.

This detection is on the far edge of the sonar. This gives direction, and distance. Too excited to write more.

#LOG 1094

Days of nothing, of just endless. Getting closer all the time. Instrumentation may not be as finely tuned as I had previously believed, however. The location of the Lilly Nora drifts a few degrees in different directions every few hours. I have slept in half-hour snatches in stretches of the deep that I can trust the vessel AI to oversee, and no more than that. I do not have the time or strength to figure out why the sonar is inaccurate. I can only describe it as shimmering.

Sonar is cold and hard information. Only something moving would displace so repetitively. Something working, or something. . .organic. I seem to shimmer myself every time the information changes. Ripples of sweat down my body, spit filling my mouth as though I am about to be sick. I am so afraid of losing her that I swear I see her. I will take her. I will claim everything in her that belongs to me. The dead do not need anything on board any longer, and I will not disturb their own graves. In the afterlife they may revolve and resolve, going from cabin to cabin and turning in circles together, swimming on the deck and dancing under it. But their things are not tangible there either. A ghost does not need a gold watch, or what precious metals and elements can be extracted from husks of electronics.

I do believe dead things should be left well enough alone.

A ship is not a dead thing.

#LOG 1103

I dream of blinking lights. Those ancient cruise liners light up like a city building. No, dream is wrong. I see them when I am awake too. I see the Lilly Nora's electronics flickering. I do not see them. I only believe I see them. I see everything and nothing through my little port hole. Awake and dreaming, I see them, and I see them open for me, like mouths, I see their secret places and the treasures within. Closer, she calls me, closer, come inside.

#LOG 1112

An Architeuthis attacked the Mitar. I was drifting forward in darkness, maintaining direction with the guidance of sonar, and adjusting when the sonar changed. It came out of nowhere, knocking me hard off course, and came with the screaming scrape and crunch of metal like bones being broken.

I do not know if the sonar could not pick it up because it was moving so fast or maybe this uncanny ability for deep sea things to evade detection is literal. It suckered its huge arms around the vessel, and I understand now that the sound I heard was its beak, sinking into the hull, hoping to find soft flesh. It must have mistaken me for prey.

I flipped the lights on, all lights, interior—exterior—posterior. That frightened the damn thing well enough, and it fled. I have dropped the Mitar to the ocean floor and anchored it. Sand like a hospital bed whilst I try to figure out the extent of the damage.

The creature looked at me before it fled. Its eye was a world all its own, the only moon I have ever seen down here.

I cursed this as a godless place when it happened, but I close my eyes and see that moon burned on my retinas. How much closer to God can I get, than being seen by the world?

#LOG 1113

There is a small remote camera I can use to view the damage. What I know for certain is that there is no hull breach. Hull damage, but no breach. There is a crucial, so crucial distinction of words there. I can see slight bowing in the cabin where the squid slammed against me with such force. I can set the Mitar to drift whilst I weld it over with spare scraps of metal, to reinforce it from the inside.

A worrisome thing. I noticed that I am drastically lower on fuel than I should be. I will not panic... but we have expended a month's worth of fuel in a matter of days. I thought the squid had damaged the fuel tanks, but the camera footage showed that all tanks were intact. There is no discernible leakage, and I checked all the internal pipes I could. It cannot be right. I do not understand. I will do a reset of the Mitar's systems in case the collision jostled the fuel meter.

It is perfectly fine. After I have explored the Lilly Nora and retrieved all that I can, I can send the Mitar back to the surface on the spot and send out a distress beacon.

#LOG 1114

When I reset the Mitar's systems, the dates leapt forward.

But it is simply ludicrous to suggest that we have been down here a month. The systems must be failing somehow, in some way that I cannot get to return to me in diagnostics.

It does not matter. I will make it not matter. I will not lose myself to whatever here picks at my anticipation and threatens to turn it into something worse, something fractious, bloody, and frightened. I must sleep.

#LOG 1118

To be asleep and to be awake are a haze. I am not sure if what I have seen is a dream or a hallucination. I saw the Lilly Nora. I took the Mitar towards her and she opened herself to me. There was a split, a seam, down the centre of her bow, and her skeletal frame groaned so loudly that the cabin shook, as the split rent itself open into a gash and with terrible screaming the bow parted open. She presented herself so beautifully, so magnificently. She made a place for me. . .but not a mouth. I went straight into her darkness.

I woke half-sprawled on my chair. The Lilly Nora is still some KM off.

#LOG 1131

Gods, what is happening down here? Is it me or the Mitar? I was shovelling a handful of those owl shit pellets and letting the AI pilot the submarine when the sonar pinged. I expected the Lilly Nora to have shimmered as she has been doing constantly, a few degrees to the directional east or west of my north.

She was south. I ran the sonar five more times. I reset all systems. She is behind me. I must turn around. Did I drift – did the Mitar drift? I am bereft of explanations, and heavy with confusion so vast it feels like grief.

There is no choice. I will turn around and go to her.

#LOG 1132

Finally. Here are the direct observations of the first human eyes to set on the Lilly Nora in a hundred years. I am positioned, stationary and at 500m, so that I might see her all. I am so afraid that if I blink or look too long at this screen she will vanish, or another temporal oddity will occur. I half expect myself to be turned about again.

Let myself describe her. The Lilly Nora appeared intact on first approach, the twelve-deck cruise liner that carried all kinds of people around the world. She was poised as a dead whale might be, tipped onto her side with her enormous hull and propellors exposed. She is in a strangely open valley of the ocean floor. I can see how she was both impossible to find yet seems impossible to miss. She is not hidden; despite her size, she is minuscule compared to the breadth of her gravesite. The ocean waters have risen since her sinking, surely contributing to how she has lain undiscovered for so long.

Appearances deceive, however. A great weight has cleaved her in half, across the middle from starboard to port, opening a cross-section of every level and the hull besides. Time has worn down what must have once been sharp, dangerous edges. Loose detritus has been swept away and more besides, giving her a skeletal look on closer inspection.

I cannot see what catastrophic thing took her down, but she must have gone down stern-first, quite dramatically too. Under enormous pressure, as she sank and the bow tipped upwards, she would have simply snapped clean in two.

Can you imagine being one of the thousands, effectively trapped within a cloistered city as the natural elements tore it apart? The enormity of their deaths. Those who did not drown will have been crushed by moving furniture, or gravity dropping them. Those who lived through that in sealed pockets of air would have died in the decompression as the ship fell to the bottom. They would not have survived any longer, and the silence that rests down here now would have taken hold.

#LOG 1137

I made more than enough observations of the Nora at a distance before I finally entered her, through that wound down her middle. I have found a stable place to rest the Mitar whilst I record my findings. I am in the stern-half.

There are bodies.

There are so many bodies, and there should not be.

I am a pirate. I have been in wrecks before, even if none were as large or deep as this. The logistics of a shipwreck are scalable. There are never human remains after this long. Putrefaction disintegrates flesh if scavenging creatures do not get there first. If the water does not carry bones away, they rarely last long enough to count. Cold delays the ruination of these corpses, but the water will erode them to nothing in time. If there was nothing, I would not be surprised. If there were some skeletal remains, I would not be surprised.

I should have started scavenging by now. I cannot bring myself to do it yet. In every room, someone looks at me. They float, suspended in toppled and destroyed rooms, arms buoyant, hair drifting around their skulls like a halo. Their eyes are open. Their jaws are slack.

#LOG 1140

I kept trying to find a room I felt comfortable pilfering from. I could not find a single room without one or more bodies in it. In the ballroom, there are dozens, all floating, all drifting, a slow dance, a performance. It is agonising to look upon. The Nora holds all its occupants close to its chest; she and she alone governs how they will rest, even as the ship itself rots.

Then something hit the side of the Mitar hard enough to cause an internal dent. Burst a pipe; I have spent the last four hours doing repairs and welds, but I cannot get the dent to push back out. The hull integrity is compromised. There is nothing in this room but a corpse. I do not know what could have hit the Mitar so hard.

#LOG 1141

The Mitar was struck by something huge. There is no Architeuthis dux to blame this time. This time the blow was so hard we were shunted into the floor of the ballroom. The dent has gotten worse, and my welds come undone. I hit my head on a jagged edge when we went down. So much blood. Outside, the others gather. It was them, I think. It must have been them. They are all looking at me, now, forming concentric semicircles around the Mitar. Perhaps the alarms of the Mitar sing to them.

I am dizzy, too dizzy to work, but conscious, to my own sorrow.

#LOG 1142

This will be my final log. My last words. It seems unlikely that anyone will ever read them, and I write for my own satisfaction. This has all been only for my own satisfaction.

Why do we call ships she and her? This is not a rhetorical question—I do not know the answer. Is it because men love them? The old joke—that ships and women are unpredictable. The rebuttal to the joke—that we can weather any storm. Is it grammatical—a stubborn habit, but an outdated feature? I have heard men talk about real women the way they do ships. Crowing after her features. Her footage, her décor. Declaring captainship, making bids to be mates. If a ship is a woman—if a ship is a person—what should we aptly call a scavenger, who arrives unwelcome into her bough?

The Lilly Nora has named me rapist. She did not want me here.

The dent has gotten worse. It will not be long now. I type this watching the many welds I have put in place over years bend and ache, pressure creeping in around me. The Mitar's wound will be deep. When she breaks, as some would say befits plunderers and violators, there will be nothing left of me to find.

WAKE
Lucas Olson

Andy was already awake when the first ghost knocked on his patio door.

Jordan rolled over, groaning, and propped herself up on her elbow.

"Andy, did you hear that?"

"Yeah," he said, swinging his legs off the bed.

tmp tmp tmp.

"Took them long enough," Jordan said. She reached for the lamp and missed twice before she hit the switch. "Uncle Mark says they've been all over the Heights already. I thought we'd missed them."

tmp tmp tmp.

The sound was muffled but walls were thin. They were the only ones in this building with a ground-floor patio. It had to be them.

Andy pulled on his sweatpants. Jordan hoisted herself into a sitting position while she watched him paw through the closet.

"I can do it if you don't want to," she said. "It might be easier."

"I'll do it," Andy said. "I remember the script." He was staring at the empty hook on their closet door. Bathrobe must still be in the wash.

"Do you want to practice?"

He turned around. Jordan had a pair of yoga

pants balled up in her hands. Waiting for him to chicken out.

"Jordan, I'm not a child."

"Alright," she said. "Okay. Just tell the truth and we won't need to think about this again."

"Right," Andy said, meaning the conversation was over.

"Right," Jordan said, meaning they understood each other.

Andy shut the bedroom door as he stepped into the hallway.

It was dark. The faint green glow of the microwave clock puddled at the end of the hallway. Andy aimed himself towards it. Each of his steps was quiet and careful. This space was still too new to him. He was always stubbing his toes. Not tonight.

Eventually the walls pulled away and he stepped into their meager, carpeted living room. Sliding glass doors connected it to the patio. The blinds were pulled shut; razor-thin slivers of moonlight sketched lines across the opposite wall.

tmp tmp tmp.

Andy laid his hand on the counter. His fingers brushed the leather knife roll. Inside, all of his chef's knives waited for Thursday. He hovered there, hesitating. There had been at least one home invasion since the wave; a burglar pretending to be a ghost.

tmp tmp tmp.

A burglar would have tried the door by now.

Andy crossed the room, stopping when his belly bumped against the blinds. He groped through the air until he found the pull chain.

Waiting.

tmp tmp—

He pulled. The blinds twisted open, pouring cold moonlight into the living room. The sight of his mother struck Andy like a hammer. His heart dropped into his stomach. She pressed a wet hand against the door and took a step closer to the light. Her blonde—*blonde?*

This wasn't his mother. The hair was wrong, and this woman was younger, nearer her fifties. She had on capris and a t-shirt with a cartoon lobster. She was drenched from head to toe, sandy-blonde hair clinging to her scalp as if for dear life.

She had no eyes.

In their place were a pair of round, grey stones. The kind rolled smooth by the ocean and piled by the tide onto less welcoming beaches.

I need dry clothes. Please, the woman said. Her want sucked the heat from the room. Behind her, a skeletal elm tree stood barely silhouetted against the night. What few stubborn leaves still clung to its branches were a sickly yellow-brown in the daylight.

"What?"

Can I borrow some dry clothes? she asked. He could feel her gaze. As though there were a force behind those stones waiting to escape. As though within the woman was something pressurized and pointed at Andy.

Please, she said. *I'm cold. I don't know where I am.*

Andy forgot everything he promised Jordan he'd remember.

"This is the Heights. Fifteen-ten Babson Heights."

Please, I can't find my car. I just need some dry clothes. Her other hand pressed against the glass. *I am so cold.*

Andy did not pull the blinds closed. The woman watched him as he backed away, but she did not knock again. Perhaps she already knew what he was doing.

There was a pile of trash bags in the laundry room, stacked beside the washer. Each had **CLOTHES TO DONATE** written on them in Andy's clumsy block lettering.

The bottom bag was from his mother's house. Winter clothes that had been binned up in the attic when the wave tossed the neighbor's Ford F-150 through the living room window. The force of it had torn through two load-bearing walls and folded up the 90-year-old house like a cardboard box. Later, they found that bin resting in the arborvitae in the backyard.

Andy was saving those. Just in case. But there must be something she could part with. He pulled out a pair of jeans and a thick sweater. When his mother still wore it, the hem fell almost to her knees.

Andy retied the knot that sealed the bag, and set the others back on top.

This woman wasn't a person, exactly. She was a lost thing, a vivid memory. He knew what he'd been told to do. But, well, he didn't see the harm, not really. He was only fulfilling a request. Perhaps when she left the absence could be a kinder one. He returned to the living room, cradling the clothes in his arms.

She was still there. The water from her hands

had left tear-streaks on the glass. As Andy undid the latch and slid open the door, a curl of frigid October air swept past him. He did not invite the woman in and she did not move to enter. She only stood there on the threshold, palms up and open.

"Here." He laid his mother's clothes in the woman's arms.

Bless you, the woman said. *Bless you.*

She turned and disappeared into the cold. Andy shut the door. After another moment staring at the darkness, he locked it, and drew the shades closed. He felt a pressure in his chest, climbing up his throat. He decided it was acid reflux.

The bedroom light was still on, but Jordan had been retaken by sleep. Andy stripped off his sweatpants and crawled back into bed. He reached over Jordan to get the light, felt the warmth of her pressed into him, and thought about the lies he'd have to tell her tomorrow.

* * *

Each morning before he opened his eyes, Andy liked to pretend it was still May. In May, he and Jordan were still in the third floor apartment at 11 Battery Square. There, he could still wake up and pass through the gentle momentum of his morning: coffee grinder, French press, eggs, cigarette, shower. He could walk to the Gillnetter, pull on his chef's coat, and begin to prep. By the time his station at sauté was clean the servers would arrive (including Jordan, on a good day). After flipping the chairs down and wiping the tables, they would open the garage doors out to the patio and though Andy was stuck behind a counter and a stack of plates he could still see the harbor beyond. Ocean air had a texture that other air did not. Back then he could still love that.

This morning, the day jumped on his chest the moment he opened his eyes. It was not a work day, so Andy would need to distract himself from himself. At the Gillnetter, he probably could have weaseled his way into seven shifts a week and been commended, but that building was a wreck now. The possible distraction of a summer rush was gone, sunken somewhere at the bottom of the harbor.

What an awful day to have off.

Jordan left a note. He folded it closed and drew a heart on the back, to spare himself seeing the words. Andy shuffled around it all morning until he settled on errands. Today would be an errands day.

Six months ago he could take a left onto Harwich Ave and be over the cut bridge in minutes. Now Harwich only carried on half a mile before ending at an alarming series of caution signs. The road had been little more than a strip of asphalt on a marsh in the first place. The heavily flood-insured houses that once lined it were now gone, each foundation left behind like the chalk outline of a body. A fishing trawler still sat sideways across the road, a strip of guard rail pinched beneath it. There was talk of leaving the boat there, as a monument.

Six months ago, Andy's mother lived on Harwich Ave. Now the spot where her garden had been was a tide pool for most of the day.

After his Chevy Impala warmed up, Andy eased it out of the parking lot and turned right. It took thirty minutes just to get onto the highway into town now, the onramp was clogged with cars. Another fifteen minutes as all those cars crammed into the single open lane, whizzing unsteadily by all the repair crews working on the road. The sight of them had been novel once.

Sun-faded detour signs were still billeted on downtown street corners. Andy parked in the lot by the library, once a townie secret, now packed every day.

CVS first (Walgreens a wet carcass). Coffee next, and an exchange with Marta, who used to give him his two large-iced-black-no-ice before work every morning. *How you doing? Oh, you know. Yeah, a beautiful service. Hanging in there. Yeah, you too.*

They didn't need groceries. Andy was going to buy them anyway. He'd cook tonight. Chowder maybe. Used to be he made chowder every morning, clams and pork belly. Maybe that would make him feel normal, relieve the pressure in him. It had climbed higher in his chest over the course of the morning. Maybe Jordan was wrong. Maybe nothing else would come of it, from just giving the ghost what it asked for. Needed.

Andy was walking fast, lost in his head. He turned quickly, headed back towards the library, and nearly collided with the ghost standing on the sidewalk. The jolt as Andy reeled back shook the lid off his coffee cup and sent cold-brew splattering onto the sidewalk.

"Jesus fuck!"

Hey, the man said. He wrapped a weak grip around Andy's wrist. He was shorter than Andy, and less bald. His baby blue polo was so soaked through Andy could see the man's dark nipples through the fabric of the shirt. He smelled like a fish left in the sun.

Hey, buddy. Do you know where the statue is? The fisherman's statue? I can't find it.

No eyes. Like the woman's they were stoppered. One stone and one mussel, deep blue and crowned with barnacles at the tip. It was slightly open, as if still underwater, and within it Andy could see the meat of the animal undulating. Was it still alive? Was it a ghost too?

Buddy?

"I'm sorry—I'm sorry, where?"

No. The statue? I can't find the statue. It's getting cold, I'd like to see it soon.

The man's hand soaked the cuff of Andy's sweatshirt.

"Head down Main Street, then take a left. That way." Andy pointed towards where the Fishermen's Memorial had been before the wave tore it from its moorings and pitched it into a Greyhound bus.

Thanks bud. Have a good day. The man's thick sneakers made a squelching sound as he walked down the slope. He made it a block before someone jumped out of a shop and chased after him, yelling that he was not supposed to be here.

* * *

No pork belly at the Star Market, so Andy used bacon. It felt nice to take the good knives back out, even if only to dice onions and potatoes. Their kitchen was small, but felt palatial compared to his station at work. He was nearly done when Jordan got home from her shift at the Liquor Locker (or was today the aesthetician classes? Andy lost track).

She stopped halfway through the sliding door. Cold air chased past her and into the kitchenette, fluttering the pages of *Outside Magazine* on the seat of the couch.

"Smells like the 'netter," she said.

Andy held his nose over the pot and let it waft in. He was working breakfasts at Lee's Place now. It had been a while since he made chowder. He hadn't meant to make the Gillnetter's recipe.

"Close? But I used a vidalia. And less thyme." He dipped his callused fingertip in and brought it to his mouth to taste, then realized he was talking shop again. "I'm sorry. I mean I didn't mean to, uh, bring that back."

"No, Andy I—" She pulled the door shut behind her. "It's soup weather. It's nice." She perched on the arm of the couch to pull off her boots, smiling at him in an old way. He smiled back, but now all he could think of was the smell. He'd been lost in the task, now he remembered how a pot full of the soup had spilled onto his work shoes as the pilings holding up the restaurant gave out.

He worked hard to smile so she'd see it.

"That's good, because it's still the only soup on the menu."

She sighed a little laugh, hung her jacket on the hook.

"Did you. . .?"

Andy tossed her a bag of oyster crackers.

"Nice."

Eating at six still felt foreign to both of them. All of Andy's shifts were openers, no nights at all for the first time in years. Jordan had never worked a job that didn't expect her there for dinner service. They were both used to 11PM leftovers. Eating dinner at the same time as the normals. Who would have thought?

They ate beside each other on the couch, watching the sky through the sliding doors. It had been aesthetician classes for Jordan today, and lunch with her mother at the house out in West Babson. Well across the canal, near the Harwich town border, perched up on a hill and ringed with pines.

"I still can't believe they haven't moved that boat," she said, running her spoon over the bottom of the bowl. She tucked the last scoop of soup into her mouth and watched him.

That had been a test and a question: *Can you talk about that road? Do you want to? Shouldn't you? Hasn't it been months?*

He would not, he did not, he didn't care.

She didn't ask about last night. Maybe she thought she was sparing him. Andy felt like there was something stuck in his throat; he wanted to get the lie out of the way but would not be the one to bring it up. He would not be able to bring it up right, so he didn't try.

There were safe and unsafe ways to remember. He knew better than to think that food could be one. He could smell it on his mustache even laying in bed. He hadn't gone back to white bean ragù or to his mother's steamed clams, why would this have been a good idea?

Every hour of Andy's sleep was punctuated by another awake, Jordan beside him snoring fretfully. At three, he decided to take their nightly water glasses back to the kitchen.

tmp tmp tmp tmp tmp tmp.

His back was to the sliding door. He could feel the force behind him slowly pressing into his spine.

tmp. tmp tmp. tmp tmp tmp. TMP.

He would have to turn around. Alright, he could do that.

Three bodies pressed against the door. Their eyes were the cloudy green and brown of sea glass. All of them were in bathing suits—two men in swim trunks and a woman in a one-piece. Their skin was blue and pruned. Seaweed and fish netting wound through one man's long hair. The woman only had one hand against the glass. The other arm ended in a seeping knob above the elbow.

Excuse me! Sir.
Hey.
Hello, do you see? Hello?

The air around Andy felt thick, humid. The woman raised her stump and slapped it against the glass door.

TMP.

They all reared their arms back again, then slapped against the glass.

Do you have any dry clothes?
It is cold as a witch's tit out here. Do you have a coat? Or something?
I can't find my bike. It was chained up on the boulevard and now I can't find it.

Can I borrow some clothes? I am soaked. A towel even, man, please.

If Andy stood there, he would start to recognize them. The voice of one he already remembered. He was on the baseball team in high school. An outfielder.

Andy? Is that Andy? Can I borrow a shirt, Andy?

He went to the laundry room, because then he would not have to watch. Once he came back he could hold his breath and they would disappear back to the darkness and leave him in peace.

* * *

"Got rid of the last of them, huh?" Jordan asked.

Andy looked up with a start. He was about to burn their tuna melts.

"Huh?" he said.

"The last of the goodwill bags. From your mom's."

"The bags are gone, yeah." There were a few things left. One outfit, barely. Just in case she showed up. Andy had it folded up in a paper grocery bag tucked behind the towels.

"I'm proud of you, for doing that. And for last week," Jordan said. "I know that wasn't easy."

"Right."

"But we did the right thing, and now it's over."

The trick to a tuna melt (or any melt, any grilled sandwich) was that you didn't actually want to use butter. Mayonnaise, spread right on the bread. It was not exactly healthier, but that detail was inconsequential. Lots of details like that were inconsequential, not worth talking about.

"Alright," Jordan said. "Well, I love you and I'll get the beer."

She poured a tallboy into two glasses and set each carefully on the floor in front of the couch. Andy cut the sandwiches into triangles with the edge of his spatula, then tucked a bag of Cheetos under his arm and grabbed the plates.

"Ooh," Jordan said. "It's snowing."

"How can you tell?" Andy looked towards the sliding doors. The shades were pulled tightly closed.

She waved her phone at him, as though he could see it from across the room, then bounced back to her feet.

"It says it's coming from the west. Do we face west?"

"I don't know," Andy said, sitting down. He knew they didn't face east. Jordan gripped the pull chain and then, softly,

tmp.

Andy froze, two plates still in hand, a glass of beer between his feet.

"It's too early," he said.

"It's November, Andrew. It snows in November sometimes." Jordan pulled the blinds open.

Their patio teemed with wet bodies. Snowflakes clung to their hair, collected on the wet fabric of their clothes. More kept coming, around the corner, over the slope. Others pressed against the tree, as though trying to catch sight of a stage. In place of all of their eyes: lead weights, bobbers, driftwood, plover eggs. Half a crab stuck out from one man, its twitching legs scratching and scratching at his nose, its claw pinching together a clump of hair.

"Mother of Christ!" Jordan said. She stumbled backwards and slammed into the wall. The force shook the hanging frames, two of which tumbled to the floor, landing face-down with a splintering crack. Jordan's feet slid out from under her.

Hello? I am very cold. Is it supposed to be so cold here this time of year?

Do you know the way to the Gillnetter? I'm certain I parked at the Gillnetter.

Jordan was looking at the crowd, but Andy could feel her focus to turn to him. The room was still. A thin dusting of snow fell from a granite-grey sky. The ghosts barely moved except to tap on the glass.

I'm all turned around.

Andy? Is that Andy? Can I borrow any dry clothes?

"Andy," Jordan said. She began, very slowly, to stand.

By the tree, was that? Maybe?

"You just—" Lumpen shapes moved on the far edge of the crowd. What had seemed like silhouetted bushes were more ghosts scaling the hill. "You made a promise, Andy!"

Do you know the time? I'm worried I might be late. I feel like I'm late.

Andy's foot kicked over both glasses of beer. What didn't seep into the carpet pooled beneath the couch.

Hello? Do you know where Russo's Marina

is? I was supposed to meet my cousin there.

"What the fuck am I supposed to do when people ask for help? What if she—"

"They aren't *people* any more, Andrew!"

I'm soaked. Can I borrow a towel? I don't need it for long.

"Listen to yourself! And you won't even answer! Coming at me like this; what would *you* do, huh?"

"Tell the fucking truth, Andy, like we said we would. I'd hoped you'd just. . .I should have done it in the first place."

Hello?

Jordan wrapped her fingers around the handle of the sliding door.

"What are you doing?" Andy asked.

I can't seem to find my house? Down on Harwich Ave? It should be right down Harwich.

That voice Andy recognized. It was the voice that taught him his name, taught him to cook.

"Jordan, wait—"

She slid open the door. The tapping stopped. The voices stopped.

"There's nothing for you here, I'm sorry!"

Andy stood. "Jordan, give me a second."

"I'm sorry that there isn't anything in here to warm you up. There isn't anywhere for you to go. I'm sorry about it, it's got nothing to do with fair. You didn't deserve it but you're dead."

Andy pushed past Jordan out into the cold. All of the ghosts were looking at them, silent. Andy saw his mother's face—he was certain that was his mother's face—just as the stones fell out of her eye sockets. All at once the ghosts came uncorked, revealing the black pits that lead back into their skulls. The water came pouring out of all of them like an unkinked hose. As it hit the air it turned to mist, then to snow.

"Wait," Andy said. The air felt sharp from all of the sudden snowflakes. They bit at his eyes until he had to look away, out of the breeze.

"Mom?" he said. "I saw you, Mom! Where are you?"

A gust of wind blew in more snow. The only voice that answered was Jordan's. The pity in it made him want to spit. He waved his arm in front of him but there was nothing to see or touch but the weather. There was no one here but the two of them.

"Mom? Where are you? I miss you!"

"Andy," Jordan said. "Please come back inside. It's okay."

Andy stumbled forward, still in his slippers. The wind picked up; the snow was getting heavier. Jordan called after him again, but the air was too soft now for the sound to travel.

"Mom?" he said. The pressure had climbed higher in him. It felt like it was going to burst out of his throat, out of his nose. The snow was blowing straight into his eyes, so he closed them. He groped forward through the blackness, through the cold. There would be an answer somewhere.

"Where are you?" he asked. "Where are you?"

THE TIDE WILL BRING THEE HOME
Dai Baddley

On a stretch of desolate coast, where only a scant few fishing hamlets are scattered, there lies a hidden cove. Only spoken of in whispers, and accessible only at low tide. In the shadow of an overhanging cliff, jagged black rocks jut along the shoreline like the spine of some great sea-serpent. If you follow these rocks until they break into the shingles, you'll see an alcove carved into the cliff, roughly eked out over centuries by human hands; it sits just high enough to escape high tide.

In this alcove lives an old man. His skin is tanned and leathered, and hangs off his bones where the flesh has long atrophied. Time and the force of countless gales have etched the wrinkles deep into his face and formed a crust of salt; his features are only clear when he opens his mouth to speak.

Not that he ever does speak, but for once every month, at full moon as the tide comes in. He raises the rusted bell at his side and, as he rings it, he croaks in the old tongue: *"This way, this way, our Lost, our Drifting, our Drowned, the tide will bring thee home."*

He sits there alone, weeping as he calls, barely audible over the crashing waves. He stares out across the sea, and his tears mingle with the water lapping at his toes.

He has sat there in that cove longer than anyone can remember, since the nearby Eglwys Oer was a thriving port town, and not the abandoned shell it is now. Generations have come and gone, and the world is smaller now, and this one man sits at the edge, forgotten. There is no one left now who remembers Aled Morgan.

* * *

"Do you ever think it's strange that we don't have a lighthouse?" Aled asked Owain, who shrugged.

"It's the way it's always been here," Owain replied. His mother's family had been in Eglwys Oer since the very beginning. Though they didn't *know* everything, they understood that some things must be.

"But don't you think, Owain, with all these rocks about and the storms we get, someone should build one?"

"Why are you worrying about this so much all of a sudden? You're not a sailor boy." Owain shook his head and smiled, that smile that first captured Aled's heart.

"I'm worrying about you."

* * *

No one knows exactly when Eglwys Oer was first settled, but it began as a small fishing settlement on the southwest coast. The church that gave the village its name was built in 1142, and it stood at the top of the grassy hill, looking down over the village, all the way down to the docks. For the next four hundred years it remained a small and isolated community, until a boom in the area's textile industry made it a convenient port.

The Morgan family arrived in the area shortly after the town's expansion. They established themselves as educated, hardworking, and good Christians, pillars of the community. Steffan Morgan was the local schoolmaster, strong and stern, while his son Aled was of a gentle nature. Aled grew up known by all in town, which is considerable pressure for a young man.

He was bookish and a good study, which suited his family well, but Aled never did play as the other boys did. He did not join in the rough-and-tumble, boxing or rugby. Eglwys Oer was always a working man's town, and it taught its men to be boisterous and burly, so Aled, for much of his childhood, faded into the background, and there was gossip that he was sickly.

When Aled began spending time with Owain, they seemed a strange pair. Owain belonged to the sea; his mother was descended from the first families of fisher-folk in the area, and his father (rumour had it) was a foreign sailor.

Owain wasn't one for school, was put to work instead, as many children were in those days. He grew up strong and bold, nipping at the heels of the sailors and visitors of Eglwys Oer's tiny port.

Aled was barely eighteen, Owain not a month older. Aled had come down to the seafront running an errand for his mother, and he stopped to observe the hustle and bustle of the culture he only nominally belonged to.

Owain was helping his friends and cousins unload the latest shipment. Working up a tremendous sweat, he opted to take his shirt off, and this was how Aled first saw him.

From behind, Aled saw that freckled back warmed to a shining gold by the sun. Muscles flexed and rippled. As if he knew eyes were upon him Owain looked around, and he smiled, and that smile was the most beautiful thing Aled had ever seen.

Owain gave him a cheeky wink and went back to his work, leaving Aled stunned not only by his beauty but his brazenness. He hung back, just in view by the storerooms, hoping that the golden sailor boy would find him. He did, and they found a hidden spot. There was barely an introduction before they were kissing, then hands fumbling down each other's trousers. It was rushed, sticky, and hot. Owain still shirtless, the heavy musk from his labours ended up imprinted on Aled's clothes. He loved it.

* * *

"Come on Aled, no one ever comes down here."

"That's the problem, I feel like we shouldn't."

"We've done a lot of things we shouldn't, love."

"I don't know, Owain."

It was a grey day, and the two of them were walking the coastal path down to the beach, in the hope of some privacy. The boys had only known each other a few weeks, but for Aled it was a lifetime. A powerful gust of wind nearly knocked them both off their feet; the path was steep and exposed, Aled yelped as he started to slip but Owain held his hand tight. Brushing his dark curls from his face and flashing that grin, Owain told him, "See? It's an adventure!"

Aled returned it with his own nervous smile, but he did not let go of Owain.

Once they set foot upon the sands, Aled looked about, to one side seeing distant ships on their way out from Eglwys Oer, and to the other a great rock formation leading up the beach, around a corner to the cliffs.

"Up that way is where Old Nain lives." Aled jumped as Owain spoke by his ear. "My mam told me about her."

"Old Nain?"

"Yes, the old woman who lives in a cave."

"The mad one?"

"You shouldn't say that." Owain was uncharacteristically serious as he told him. "She's been here a long time, and my mam told me she looks out for us."

Sailors are a superstitious folk, and Owain was no exception.

"I'm sorry love." Aled turned and kissed him on the cheek. Owain kissed him back "Let's not worry about that now."

They lay down under that darkening sky and made love, entirely forgetting themselves until they felt the encroaching waves splashing their feet.

Owain was the first to pull away from their embrace, jumping to his feet. "Tide's coming in!" Adjusting his clothes, he hopped from one foot to another, playfully splashing Aled.

"It's in my eyes, you bastard!" Aled swatted at him but laughed anyway, and propped himself up on his elbows. After their exertions, the cool breeze and chilly water felt good on his skin.

As Owain began to make his way back up to the path, Aled gazed out to the water. It was so different, away from the docks and the boats and the people, so quiet.

The sky reflected black in the surf, the rolling waves merged with the clouds. Even here at the shore the water appeared bottomless under this shroud.

He was dimly aware of Owain calling to him, but Aled was mesmerised by the sea. Under the crash and rumble, he began to hear a voice. No, voices. Starting as the faintest murmur, they grew louder as more seemed to join the chorus. They were crying and weeping, calling out as if they knew Aled was listening.

"Aled! Aled, come on mun, you don't want to be swept away-" Owain's words were cut off by a cry of pain as he came running back, which brought Aled back to his senses. He looked around to see Owain back on the ground, clutching his bloodied foot.

"What happened?" Aled scrambled over.

"Slipped on fucking rock," Owain muttered through gritted teeth. His sole was split like a ripe fruit, the cut deep and bleeding profusely.

"Can you stand? I'll support you back home." Aled gripped Owain's wrist and pulled him up.

"Carry me like a blushing bride, will you?" Owain laughed, then hissed as he instinctively put his foot down into the sand and salt water. As the blood seeped out and water seeped in, Aled thought he heard the voices starting up again.

But he had no time to dwell on it, the tide was coming in rapidly, so he pulled Owain to his side and held him as he hobbled along. When they finally reached the dirt path, Aled looked back and saw a figure sitting on one of the distant rocks, the rushing water swirling around them.

* * *

From the top of the cliff, Aled squinted at the horizon, sure he could see the ships. One of them was carrying Owain. This was his first big journey, and he couldn't have been more excited. The ocean was in his blood, and he was made to see the world.

He was so proud of himself when he told Aled, "We're sailing all the way to London! First Penzance, then Southampton, then the big city! I've been brushing up on my English with the other lads."

Owain had only been out on the fishing boats before, afraid to leave his mother behind, but he was a grown man now. Exotic places and peoples awaited him, and Aled would wait faithfully behind.

He would wait.

The ships faded, first to dots, then they were gone. And Aled found himself completely alone. A chill wind picked up and he shivered, pulling his coat tight around himself. The wind whistled in his ears, biting with the cold. He tried to bury his head in his scarf. The force of the wind increased, the whistle rising and rising until all of a sudden it transformed into a human-sounding wail.

Aled startled, then stumbled, tripping over his

own feet and landing with a thud and a gasp on the very edge of the cliff. He gripped the short grass, digging his nails into the earth in panic. His head hung over the edge and he found himself staring down into the surf as it broke on the pebbles. The voices called to him again, neither in Welsh nor English but the language of grief. The words were comprehensible not to the ears but to the heart, and they made Aled's pound and ache as if to burst from the speaker's pain. He wanted to get away, but the wind was blowing almost to a gale and it pinned him in place.

Terrified, Aled tried to cry out, and tears stung at his eyes, dropping into the saltwater below, which foamed and rushed at the shore. Faces formed in the bubbles and gaped up at Aled, tendrils of seaweed became digits clawing at the surface, trying desperately to reach the land. Aled stared and the Drowned returned his gaze, they knew him now and knew he saw them. With their collective force the waves rose and churned, and now Aled knew this could not be a natural storm.

He tried to shut his eyes, they were hurting. His heart was hurting. It was so cold, and he was so afraid.

A bell.

Faintly, so faintly, a bell rang out, then was joined by a woman's voice. Far below, hidden by the cliff, Old Nain sang her song to soothe the Drowned. Their wails grew to a scream, then slowly subsided. Once the cold wind had settled back down to a breeze, Aled scrambled back from the edge and to his feet. He was so shaken he had forgotten for a moment about Owain.

Owain, out on the water, in the storm.

* * *

Owain's trip was supposed to last a few weeks. Aled knew this, he knew it, but after the storm at the cliff the voices were there, whispering in his ear in their mournful tongue that Owain was gone, he was one of them now.

At home, he heard the whispering. At the schoolhouse, where he taught the young boys, he heard the whispering. Though none knew the cause, Aled's distraction was obvious to all around him. He constantly twitched and brushed his ears, as if batting away a fly. He stopped eating (to his mother's consternation) and grew thin. Often, his family could see he had been crying. His father dismissed this as some passing thing, but after two weeks his mother attempted to reach him.

"Aled, my love, we thought you were happy, you'd always been such a quiet boy and then all of a sudden you were always going out and smiling. What happened?" In his room, she sat beside him on the bed, rubbing his arm comfortingly.

"I..." he started. "I'm sorry, Mam." He began to weep again. He felt her love, but he couldn't tell her the truth. She watched him cry and accepted his silence, but stayed with him, at his side.

* * *

Owain should have been back by now. Six weeks had passed, and despite his fear Aled returned to the clifftop. He shook not from the cold, but from nerves, but he had to see Owain come back. He strained his eyes to look out again at the horizon, praying to see those dots return and grew bigger and ship-shaped.

He's gone. Aled didn't want to believe it, but there were no ships approaching. He left you that first day. That sudden storm, the voices. They were louder now, but fortunately no storm.

The peals of the bell began again from the bottom of the cliff, and the woman's voice, they could be heard so much clearer now. Now Aled realised it could only be Old Nain. Mad Old Nain, who lived alone on the rocky shore, who looked after Eglwys Oer.

Old Nain who sang to the Drowned.

He had to speak to her. He whipped around and broke into a run, to find the path down to the beach. It was only when he arrived at the top, huffing and wheezing, that he saw it was high tide, and he would have to wait until the water receded.

* * *

At low tide, when night had drawn in, Aled sneaked out from his home and back to the beach. He had only a candle to light his way, and he guarded it carefully against the wind. He crept to the cove, and found the spiny rock formation that pointed the way. Candlelight reflected in the smooth stone surface that Aled almost thought it to be a mirror.

He followed it until he felt his shoes crunching gravel rather than sand, and the shadow of the cliff sheltered him from the worst of the elements. He held his candle at arm's length and peered into the darkness, searching for any sign of life. Just outside the flickering light there was a rustle. Aled jumped back and cried out, then he saw, sitting above him before a small alcove forming barely more than a scrape in the rock, the oldest woman he had ever seen.

With her watery eyes Old Nain looked down at him indifferently. Those eyes were blue dots buried in a sea of deep wrinkles, the skin hanging off her face and pulling it down, emphasising her hollow cheeks. Her brow was set in a permanent furrow, the corners of her mouth pointed down, but her aura was one of sorrow, not anger. The only part of her that was smooth was her scalp, clearly visible as she had just a few wispy locks of hair left. One could tell she had once been a matronly woman, as her current thinness did not suit her. She had wept for years and wasted away, somehow Aled knew as he regarded her back.

He took a deep breath, and braved to speak. "Old Nain? I've come to speak with you."

She gave no response. Then he remembered his manners.

"My name is Aled Morgan."

At that, she sighed and uncurled herself from her sitting position. Slowly, with grunts of effort, she clambered down from her perch.

When finally she landed, she extended a liver-spotted hand and touched Aled's clothes. "There were no Morgans last I was in the village." She spoke so quietly, Aled had to lower his head to hear. "You were with the other boy, who gave his blood to the tide." She paused and shook her head. "I'm sorry."

"You're talking about Owain? He's a sailor."

"He cut his foot on the rock, and the sea tasted his blood." Old Nain met his eyes.

"You saw? That day on the beach?" The blood rose to his cheeks with a rush of embarrassment at what else she might have seen, but the old woman made no further comment. Swallowing that feeling, he decided to press her. "You know about the voices? The faces in the sea?"

"They are only people. The ones who die at sea, they come here. They had no proper burial, no hallowed ground, and they are trapped in the depths." She turned her head and he followed her gaze out to the waters. The seaweed again seemed to push to break the surface, and human faces formed to cry out to them. Old Nain began to hum, and the sea-ghosts dissipated once again. "Does the church still stand?" she asked suddenly.

"Yes," Aled whispered back, still staring at the waves.

"The church is a token, a small comfort. The people go to pray for their lost loved ones, their fishermen and their sailors, all lost on the treacherous rocks and endless storms. But they never built a lighthouse, did they?"

Aled shook his head.

"There must be a sacrifice, you see. We let go of a few of our own, and we get to call home the rest. Your boy is gone."

"No," Aled choked out, anger and grief filling him.

"He was gone when he set sail during the storm. The sea tasted his blood, and now it has claimed him. Now it has tasted your tears, and it has claimed you. It claimed me before, and now it will let me go." She paused. "I'm sorry."

The young man felt the truth of her words and it crushed him. Bitterly, he spoke through his tears. "Owain said you look after us."

"The seamen? I do, I soothe their souls and call them home. My sacrifice, however unwilling, allows me the bell and its song." She hummed again her lullaby for the lost, a balm for the restless souls. In her mind she saw, so long ago, a tiny fishing boat bearing a husband and two sons, caught in a tempest, and capsized. "Now I will see them again," she said aloud, then turned to Aled. "And you will see yours too, when the next comes to relieve you of this duty."

Old Nain then produced the bell from her ragged dress and held it out to Aled. "You will know the song. When high tide approaches, call out to them, the Lost, the Drifting, and the Drowned. Let the tide carry them home. You will see your man again one day."

* * *

So Aled Morgan took his place in that alcove under the cliff. In Eglwys Oer at first there were questions, but the old families understood. Over time this was accepted, and it was as if he was never there, the schoolmaster's boy who always stood apart. The world moved on, generations born and died, and new, larger ports sprung up, like Cardiff to the east, to accommodate the rapid growth of the coal and steel industries. The people moved away from Eglwys Oer, and an old man sits there alone, hoping always for his lover's reunion, unaware that there comes no successor. But still people venture out to sea, and still they lose their lives to it, so their ghosts still swim to that abandoned coast, lured by old Morgan's words: "The tide will bring thee home."

I FLOAT
Gerri Leen

Invisible
Or so small you can't see me
Silent
Although once I'd have crunched
If you stepped on me
Or tossed me into a bin
Instead of the water

To call me plastic
Is far too simple
To call me inert
Is to misunderstand how the energy
Of so many can be
Infused into a thing
Even one
As micro as I

And today, I feel female
Although I can be anything
Or nothing or all things
But I feel maternal
I play with the Humpback
And her baby as they suck in
The plankton and me, so much
Of me

I brush against a mother yellowfin
She ingests one fish, then two
All full of me or part of me

There is so much of me
Pronouns become confusing
You love to eat her kind
Raw or cooked—suck me in

As she slowly dies without knowing it
And you, who tossed me here
Know you will die but seem not to care—
Or not enough to have stopped me
While you still could—
It seems unfair that it will take me
So much longer to get to you
Than to these innocents
But that's the way of the world
And I can't change what I am
Even if I change how I am
Soon I'll be too small to clean
Already too small to pick up
In most cases

At least I will remember you
All the places I was useful
Or convenient or just annoyingly
Omnipresent, even when you'd have
Preferred a safer alternative
I recall laughter at your parties
The sobs at a sad movie
The happiness of the right result on
An early pregnancy test
They are all in me; I am in all of them
Now I feel...nostalgic and sad
I'll float off—this part of
The larger me—and let you be
But I'm never far
Don't fear that I'll desert you
It's too late for that

Author Biographies

Dai Baddley is a queer trans writer from Wales, and is inspired by myths and superstitions of his home country. He is currently training as an archivist at Aberystwyth University, but can be found haunting a shoreline near you. This is his first published work of fiction.

Grace Daly (she/her) is an author with an invisible chronic illness. She has been published in the 'Rewired' horror anthology by Ghost Orchid Press, as well as in MIDLVLMAG and JMWW. She lives near Chicago, Illinois and spends most of her time with her dog, who is a very good boy. She can be found at GraceDalyAuthor.com, or @GraceDalyAuthor for Twitter and Instagram.

Ariel Dodson writes horror, weird, fantasy and mystery fiction for adults and teenagers. Her short fiction has been published in Ellery Queen Mystery Magazine, Dark Lane Anthology, A-Z of Horror series (F is for Fear and J is for Jack o'Lantern), and Women of Horror series (Don't Break the Oath). She is the author of Blood Moon, a novel inspired by a 16th century werewolf legend, and the Southmore fantasy series for teenagers involving magic, jewels and an ancient family curse.

Daphne Fama is a lawyer turned writer, who spent long weeks in spring in her mother's seaside town in the Philippines. She jumped off the end of the pier there to prove to the boys that she was just as brave as them. That pier is long gone and so are the fishermen who laughed when she first took that leap.

Alicia Hilton is an author, editor, arbitrator, professor, and former FBI Special Agent. She believes in angels and demons, magic, and monsters. Her work has appeared or is forthcoming in Akashic Books, Channel, Daily Science Fiction, Eastern Iowa Review, Lovecraftiana, Modern Haiku, Neon, NonBinary Review, Space and Time, Spectral Realms, Unnerving, Vastarien, World Haiku Review, Year's Best Hardcore Horror Volumes 4, 5 & 6, and elsewhere. She is a member of the Horror Writers Association, the Science Fiction and Fantasy Poetry Association, and the Science Fiction and Fantasy Writers Association. Her website is aliciahilton.com. Follow her on Twitter @aliciahilton01

Miranda Johansson is a writer from northern Sweden. She has been telling stories all her life, but only recently decided to turn her passion into a career. Her short story Holden Ledge is her first professionally published work. She can be found on Twitter @highwaybones

Gerri Leen lives in Northern Virginia and originally

hails from Seattle. In addition to being an avid reader, she's passionate about horse racing, tea, and collecting encaustic art and raku pottery. She has stories and poems in The Magazine of Fantasy & Science Fiction, Nature, Strange Horizons, Galaxy's Edge, Dark Matter, Daily Science Fiction, and others, and has a poetry collection coming out from Trouble Department. She's a member of SFWA and HWA. See more at gerrileen.com

H.M. Lightcap lives in a small town in Pennsylvania. She works at a small nonprofit and goes to a community college. Her hobbies include reading, writing, watercolor painting, and photography.

Noah Lloyd is a writer of dark fantasy and speculative fiction, including the paranormal mystery podcast Burgess Springs, which was somehow, briefly, the #1 drama podcast in New Zealand. Noah holds a PhD. in English literature from Cornell University and now lives and works in Boston. You can follow him on Twitter @noahghola and read their interviews with writers of all stripes at noah-lloyd.com

Elizabeth R. McClellan is a white disabled gender/queer demisexual poet writing on unceded Quapaw and Chickasha Yaki land in what settlers call the Mid-South. In kans other life, ka is a domestic and sexual violence attorney working with refugee and immigrant survivors. Kans work has appeared in Nightmare Magazine, Strange Horizons, Apex Magazine, Eternal Haunted Summer, Utopia Science

Fiction, Apparition Lit, Illumen Magazine, Kaleidotrope, Rejection Letters, The Dread Machine, Mirror Dance, and many others, including the MOTHER: TALES OF LOVE AND TERROR anthology available now from Weird Little Worlds Press. Kans work is forthcoming in the THERE USED TO BE A HOUSE HERE anthology in 2023. They can be found on most social media as popelizbet and on Patreon as ermcclellan

Taliesin Neith (he/they) was born in 1994, and grew up fascinated by all things morbid and grotesque. When he isn't daydreaming about monsters beyond human comprehension, they spend their time with their pet cats, playing video games, building keyboards, and working on digital art. He can be found on twitter @cadavertrial

Lucas Olson is a horror writer from coastal Massachusetts. Their fiction or poetry has previously appeared in Perhappened and the Golden Key, among others. They are currently writing their first novel. More of their work can be found at lucasolsonwriter.com

H.V. Patterson (she/her) lives in Oklahoma, USA. She writes horror poetry and fiction. Her poem, Mother; Microbes (previously published in Monstroddities from Sliced Up Press), was selected for Brave New Weird: The Best New Weird Horror from Tenebrous Press. She's also been published by Dread Stone Press, Shacklebound Books, Creature Publishing, and Etherea Magazine. She promotes women in horror through Dreadfulesque (@Dreadfulesque on Twitter and Instagram), and you can follow her on Twitter @ScaryShelley and Instagram @hvpattersonwriter

Marisca Pichette wanders the border between sea and shore, searching the shadows for fragments of creatures lost. More of her work can be found in Strange Horizons, Fantasy Magazine, and Vastarien, among others. Her debut poetry collection, Rivers in Your Skin, Sirens in Your Hair, is coming in April 2023 from Android Press. Find her on Twitter @MariscaPichette and Instagram @marisca_write

Melissa Pleckham is a Los Angeles-based writer, actor, and musician. Her work has been featured in or is forthcoming from Rooster Republic Press, Timber Ghost Press, Flame Tree Fiction, Hungry Shadow Press, Luna Luna, Mind's Eye Publications' The Vampiricon, Head Shot Press' Bang! An Anthology of Noir Fiction, and more. She is a member of the Horror Writers Association. She also plays bass and sings for the garage-goth duo Black Lullabies. Find her online at melissapleckham.com or on social media at @mpleckham

JP Relph is a working-class Cumbrian writer, mostly hindered by four cats and aided by copious tea. She volunteers in a charity shop where they let her dress mannequins and have first dibs on haunted objects. A forensic science degree and passion for microbes, insects and botany often influence her words. Recently found in Noctivagant Press, Molotov

Cocktail and Reflex Fiction. @RelphJp

Christopher Sartin lives in the United States. He specifically hails from the hollows of southern West Virginia where monsters and madness are as common as the black rock that runs through the state's veins. He is a licensed social worker, working with at-risk youth. He shares his humble abode with his beautiful wife, daughters, and canine conspirator Milo.

Max Turner is a gay transgender man based in the United Kingdom. He is also a parent, nerd, intersectional feminist and coffee addict. Max writes speculative and science fiction, fantasy, furry fiction, many sub-genres of horror, and LGBTQ+ romance and erotica. More often than not, he writes combinations thereof. Max's website is maxturneruk.com

A.J. Van Belle is a writer and scientist whose short fiction has appeared in journals and anthologies from 2004 to the present. Their novels are represented by Lauren Bieker of FinePrint Literary Management. As a biologist, they draw on their science background to inform the world-building details in their fiction. They can be found on Twitter @ajvanbelle or at ajvanbelle.com

Davis Walden (he/they) is a writer, actor, and sound designer based in Portland, Oregon. He has been published by The NoSleep Podcast and The Wicked Library and is a sound designer for Nightlight and Victoria's Lift. When he isn't writing or reading,

Davis enjoys playing Dungeons & Dragons, watching documentaries, and going out for runs. You can find out more by following @daviswaldeniv on TikTok/Instagram/Twitter or by visiting daviswalden.com

Editor Biography

Elle Turpitt is a writer and editor from a seaside town in South Wales. She loves the sea, despite almost drowning twice. She co-edited the anthology A Woman Built By Man, runs Divination Hollow Reviews and is producer and co-host for Esbat: A Bookish Podcast. Her short stories have appeared in *The Dead Inside*, *Were Tales*, and on The NoSleep Podcast. You can follow her on Twitter @elleturpitt and find out more about her editing work at elleturpittediting.com

Trigger Warnings

The following list isn't exhaustive, but it takes into account certain themes and situations included in *Sand, Salt, Blood:*

- Assault (non-sexual)
- Blood / gore
- Claustrophobia
- Climate collapse
- Death of a parent/death of a partner
- Decomposition
- Domestic violence
- Drowning
- Dysphoria
- Eye trauma
- Graphic depictions of bodies
- Homophobia
- Loss / theft of a child
- Mental health issues
- Pregnancy & childbirth
- Shark attack
- Suicide
- Surgery / surgery reversal
- Thalassophobia
- Transphobia
- Violence against animals

Printed in Great Britain
by Amazon